# JOSS WOOD

---

# ONE NIGHT TO FOREVER

Recycling programs
for this product may
not exist in your area.

ISBN-13: 978-1-335-97152-4

One Night to Forever

**Printed in U.S.A.**

# It had taken every ounce of his willpower to wrench his eyes off Lachlyn's exquisite face.

Not something he generally had a problem with.

Women liked him and he liked women, when he had time for them. He usually didn't; growing a business took all his energy and what little free time he did have that wasn't spent with his friends—particularly the Ballantynes—was taken up by his demanding sisters and slightly neurotic mother.

But his *me-time* was finally here. His business was established. His family was, for all intents and purposes, off his hands, at least for the next two weeks.

Freedom couldn't come soon enough. He was going to party hard and date wild women, women who knew the score, who wanted nothing more than a good time.

The thought that he might be wanting wild because he was avoiding love and commitment jumped into his head. He was self-aware enough to realize that his quest for me-time went deeper than a simple desire to walk on the wild side. He prided himself on being responsible and part of that responsibility was not subjecting any woman to the chance that he might, like his dad, fail at a relationship.

He'd never failed in his life and he didn't intend to start now.

So, for all those reasons and more, dating Linc's new sister wasn't an option.

* * *

*One Night to Forever* is part of the Ballantyne Billionaires series from Joss Wood!

Dear Reader

The Ballantyne series was originally four books, three brothers—Jaeger, Beck and Linc—and their sister Sage. They each had their place in the family, but while I was writing Beck's story, they kept telling me that someone was buying up shares in their worldwide gem company. I figured out Tyce, my hero from *Little Secrets: Unexpectedly Pregnant*, was the culprit but why?

Because this series explores family in all its many forms, I gave Tyce a sister, who happens to be Connor Ballantyne's biological daughter. Tyce bought the shares as a gift to his sister, Lachlyn. This is her story. And Reame's, the broody, hot-as-fire former Special Forces agent turned security specialist who is Linc's best friend.

It was so much fun pulling these two stubborn people together to complete the Ballantyne family. By the way, I'd love to one day write Shaw's story. He's a terror at five and he's going to be a heartbreaker at thirty-five! Writing about the Ballantynes has been a blast—I'm very sad to let them go.

Happy reading,

*Joss*

xxx

Connect with me on my website: www.josswoodbooks.com; Twitter: @josswoodbooks; Facebook: Joss Wood Author

**Joss Wood** loves books and traveling—especially to the wild places of southern Africa. She has the domestic skills of a potted plant and drinks far too much coffee.

Joss has written for Harlequin KISS, Harlequin Presents and, most recently, the Harlequin Desire line. After a career in business, she now writes full-time. Joss is a member of the Romance Writers of America and Romance Writers of South Africa.

### Books by Joss Wood

### Harlequin Desire

*Convenient Cinderella Bride*

### *The Ballantyne Billionaires*

*His Ex's Well-Kept Secret*
*The Ballantyne Billionaires*
*The CEO's Nanny Affair*
*Little Secrets: Unexpectedly Pregnant*
*One Night to Forever*

Visit her Author Profile page at Harlequin.com, or josswoodbooks.com, for more titles.

To Rebecca Crowley: book sister,
fellow writer and sounding board.
I'm going to miss you and your wicked SOH!
Remember: when in doubt, drink wine.

# One

Lachlyn Latimore walked into the hallway of what was perhaps the most famous brownstone in Manhattan, possibly the world. Known to New Yorkers as The Den, it was five stories of weathered brick, owned and lived in by multiple generations of the Ballantyne family.

The family she was apparently linked to by DNA.

Lachlyn politely thanked Linc Ballantyne when he took her vintage coat and draped it over the back of a chaise longue chair to the right of the wood and stained glass front door. Lachlyn hoped that he didn't notice the coat's frayed pocket or missing button.

Lachlyn folded her arms across her plain white long-sleeved top and resisted the urge to wipe her damp hands on her black skinny jeans. As the newly discovered, illegitimate daughter of Connor Ballantyne, who'd been jeweler to the world's richest and most powerful people and a Manhattan legend, she had a right to feel intimidated. Connor might have passed years ago but his children were as influential and celebrated as their late father.

Lachlyn darted a glance at the portrait of Connor situated on the wall directly opposite the grand staircase. She'd inherited Connor's blue eyes, bright blond hair, that straight, fine nose. She had her mom's tiny build and wide, full mouth but the rest of her was, dammit, pure Ballantyne.

"Thanks for coming over, Lachlyn. Let's go down to the family room," Linc suggested and gestured her to follow him, but before they could move, the doorbell rang.

Linc sent her an apologetic look. "Sorry, that's my son's babysitter." Retracing his steps, he placed his hand on the carved newel post and called up the stairs. "Shaw? Reame is here."

Linc flipped open the lock to the front door and Lachlyn watched a very tall man step into the hallway to immediately dominate the space. Now, that was a hell of a babysitter, Lachlyn thought. While Linc and the sexy stranger did that half handshake, half hug men did, Lachlyn made a bullet list of the sexy stranger's attributes: caramel-colored hair, tanned olive skin, golden scruff on his jaw. Wide shoulders, narrow hips and a fairly spectacular ass...

She wasn't one to normally notice men's butts, so this was new. His eyes—a clear, light green— touched her face and she felt like she was all woman, utterly desirable. Lachlyn searched for air, found none and decided breathing didn't matter if she had him to look at. She felt alive, sexy, in tune and in touch with every spark of femininity she possessed. He oozed confidence and capability and God, he made her feel alive.

So this was that thing they called sexual attraction. Hot, pulsing, making her ache with a need to touch and be touched. He looked like a modern-day Sir Galahad, the original white knight: strong, capable, decisive and sexy enough to turn medieval and modern-day female heads.

He wasn't her type, though. In order to have a type, you had to be interested in dating, men and relationships.

Hearing a yell from above their heads, Lachlyn dragged her eyes from his muscled thighs—what were her eyes doing down there?—and looked up to watch a young boy dash down the stairs. From five steps up, the child threw himself into the air and Lachlyn released a terrified gasp, convinced that his small body would make contact with the floor. She stumbled forward but before she could make any progress, the tall man caught the child and tucked him under his arm like a football.

Lachlyn placed her hand on her heart and closed her eyes. Holy crap, she'd thought the kid was going to end up splattered all over the wooden floor.

"You've got to stop doing that, Shaw," Linc stated, not looking or sounding worried. In fact, of the three of them, she seemed to be the only one who was remotely concerned about blood, broken bones or stitches.

Linc gestured to Lachlyn. "Reame, meet Lachlyn Latimore. Lachlyn, Reame Jepsen is my oldest friend. And he's holding my son, Shaw."

The man dropped Shaw to his feet and their eyes collided. Whoosh—there went the air in the room. Again.

"Ms. Latimore."

His voice was deep and held just a hint of gravel, a touch of rasp. Lachlyn wanted to know what his words felt like as they hit her bare skin... He held out a hand and she could easily imagine it gliding over her hip, cupping her breast. Lachlyn felt lava flow into her cheeks and ignored his broad, masculine hand. She didn't trust herself to touch him. She wasn't going to risk spontaneously combusting and setting Linc's hallway alight.

"Hi," she muttered, looking down at her shoes.

"Hi back." Yeah, she heard the amusement in his words. Lachlyn forced her eyes up and...yep, she caught his quick smirk. Reame Jepsen liked the effect he had on women and wasn't even a tiny bit surprised by her ridiculous reaction. Usually that smirk would be a total turn-off but instead of being repulsed, she found his self-confidence attractive. Even alluring.

Oh, man. Not good. In fact, very, very bad.

"Unca Reame!"

Reame's eyes left her face—thank God, she felt pinned to the floor—to look down at Shaw, who was hanging on to his bulging-with-muscles arm. *Oh, stop it, Lachlyn!* Shaw monkey-climbed up the side of Reame's body, eventually settling on Reame's hip. Lachlyn watched as Shaw lifted his top lip to show Reame a bloody gap in his mouth.

"I losth my tooth," Shaw lisped.

"I see that," Reame replied. "You look gross."

Shaw grinned before scowling. "The tooth fairy forgot to come."

Standing behind Shaw, Linc grimaced and rolled his eyes. Lachlyn might not know a lot about kids but it was obvious that someone forgot to leave cash under Shaw's pillow. "Bummer. The tooth fairy who services this area must be a bit of a slacker," Reame said, managing to keep his face straight.

"Mom said it's because I didn't pick up my toys and that the tooth fairy is probably a girl and girl fairies don't like messy rooms," Shaw said, looking disgusted.

"Maybe that's it."

There was nothing sexier than watching a handsome man interacting with a cute kid, Lachlyn decided. They could easily be part of a TV commercial and would sell the advertised product by the caseload.

"Try again tonight, bud," Reame suggested and Lachlyn's lips quirked at the *don't you dare forget* look he sent Linc.

"Can we go already?" Shaw whined, tugging on Reame's arm.

Reame nodded and Lachlyn saw the smile he directed at the young boy. It was open and affectionate and ten times more powerful than his earlier smirk.

It was obvious that he enjoyed Linc's son and Linc seemed fully comfortable in handing Shaw into his care. Since everyone in the city knew that Linc was a devoted and protective father, he had to have complete faith that Reame would keep Shaw safe. That was, Lachlyn realized, a hell of an endorsement. Jepsen might look like a sports model but Linc trusted him with his son so that meant he had to have some skills.

Lachlyn listened as Linc and his friend confirmed arrangements for dropping Shaw off and within thirty seconds, the gorgeous man and the gregarious boy were gone and she was alone with Linc.

She wanted to know who Reame was and how he fit into Linc's life. So, strangely for her, she asked.

"I've known him all my life. We lived in the same neighborhood as young kids," Linc replied. "My mom got the job as Connor's housekeeper and we moved into this house but, despite living totally different lives on opposite sides of the city, Reame and I remained friends."

She shouldn't ask anything more, but no man had ever affected her the way Reame had and, well, she was curious. "Does he work for you, at Ballantyne International?"

"God, no, we'd kill each other." Linc shook his head, seemingly at ease with her questions. "Reame owns a security consulting company. He was in the military, in one of those hush-hush units that did hush-hush things. He has a hell of a military record, including some hefty commendations for bravery.

For a couple of years, I didn't see or hear from him for months at a time. That's the life these Special Forces guys lived. Then…" Linc hesitated and Lachlyn gave him a sharp look. He wasn't going to stop talking now, was he?

"Then?" Lachlyn prompted, accompanying the question with a mental slap.

"He had a crisis in his family and he needed to come home. His mom and sisters needed him. He left the military and started work as Connor's bodyguard. He's a natural entrepreneur, so after picking up more clients, he started employing his military friends as bodyguards and his security business was born. Add in cheating spouse investigations and cyber security for corporations, and Jepsen & Associates is one of the biggest security companies in the city," Linc said, sounding proud.

Beauty, brawn and brains. It was a good thing that she'd never see him again; the man was trouble.

Big, beautiful trouble.

Walking away from The Den, Reame slowed his steps so that Shaw didn't have to jog to keep up with him. "So, want to tell me why you sent me an SOS message? I thought we agreed that you can only use that message for emergencies."

Reame hadn't been worried when he received the "help me" picture-message sent from Tate's phone two hours earlier since he'd been on a call with Linc at the time and knew that everything was fine at The Den.

"It was an emergency. Spike wanted you to take me to the batting cages."

*Yeah, right.* "An emergency is when someone is hurt, or there's a fire or there's blood. Not a message about baseball from a bearded dragon, Shaw," Reame told his godson. "Does Tate know that you used her phone?"

Tate was Linc's fiancée and the reason his best mate now walked around with a dopey, having-great-sex look on his face. Actually, all the Ballantyne men had lucked out with their women. It was strange to see his childhood friends settled down. It wasn't that long ago that they were all running around Manhattan, enjoying their status as the island's most eligible bachelors. But recently, each of them had fallen and fallen hard. Reame, a die-hard bachelor and commitment-phobe, had laughed his ass off.

He liked Piper, Cady and Tate and respected his friends' choices. But settling down wasn't something he was interested in. The thought of placing himself in that situation caused his throat to close and his stomach to cramp.

Marriage, the emotional equivalent of antifreeze…

Pulling his attention back to Shaw, Reame realized that he had yet to answer his question. "Well?"

"Kind of."

That meant no. Before Reame could chastise him, Shaw turned those big blue eyes on him. "It was a 'mergency, Uncle Ree. I would've had to go to Auntie Piper's house 'cause dad wanted to talk to that lady.

And I'd have to play with the babies," Shaw complained. "Since you were only working, I thought we could hang out."

Only working… If that's what he could call running a multimillion-dollar international security business. "I needed you to save me from playing with the babies," Shaw stated dramatically.

Master manipulator, Reame thought, but, damn, he was cute. Reame sighed and shook his head. He'd survived brutal training, fought in intense battles both in war and in the boardroom, but he was putty in Shaw's hands. The reality was that if Shaw—or any of the Ballantynes—called he'd drop everything. They were family. It was what they did.

"That lady was pretty," Shaw said, cleverly changing the subject.

Pretty? No. She was heart-stoppingly, spine-tinglingly beautiful and he hadn't had such a primitive reaction to a woman in, well, years. Possibly not ever.

Reame looked down into the mischievous face of his godson and lifted his eyebrows. "Aren't you a little young to be noticing pretty girls?" he asked.

Shaw wrinkled his nose, bunching his freckles together. God, he loved this kid. "She's my Grandpa Connor's real daughter. But she wasn't 'dopted by him, like Dad was."

"So I heard, bud."

When the Ballantynes first heard of Lachlyn's possible connection to their family—thanks to her brother, Tyce Latimore—Reame had immediately ordered his best investigator to dig into her life. On paper, she seemed like nothing special. She lived alone, worked at the New York Public Library, seemed to keep to herself. Nothing about her raised any flags but looking at the photo in the file, his stomach had flipped. Back then, for some reason, and although he'd yet to meet her, she'd bothered him. Despite not knowing anything about her except that she was Connor's daughter, she'd made him feel queasy, unsettled.

The same instinct that had saved his ass on many hot situations as a Special Forces operative had screamed that Lachlyn Latimore would have some impact on his life.

Meeting her hadn't done anything to quiet the raging bats-on-speed in his stomach, Reame thought, keeping a light hand on Shaw's shoulder as they walked to a baseball center a few blocks away from The Den. The photos in Lachlyn's file hadn't done her justice. Her eyes and face were Connor's but her eyes were a deeper blue, almost violet, her face finer, her cheekbones more pronounced, and her mouth looked like it was made to be kissed. She was tiny, she barely reached his shoulder, but curvy and strung tighter than a steel guitar.

It had taken every ounce of his willpower to wrench his eyes off her exquisite face in order to catch Shaw's midair flight. Reame shuddered, thinking that if he'd taken a second longer to react, Shaw would have hit the deck at lightning speed. The kid really had to stop thinking he was a superhero. Or

Reame had to keep his concentration around pretty women.

Not something he generally had a problem with.

Women liked him and he liked women, when he had time for them. He usually didn't; running and growing a business took all his energy and what little free time he did have that wasn't spent at work or with his friends—particularly the Ballantynes—was taken up by his demanding sisters and slightly neurotic mother.

But his *me-time* was finally here. His business was established enough and his staff competent enough for him to step back a fraction, freeing up some precious spare time. His family was also, for all intents and purposes, off his hands. For ten years, since his father had decided to go AWOL after twenty-five years of marriage, he wasn't his mother's and sisters' sounding board, their bank manager, the payer of bills. His youngest sister was starting a new job next week and that meant, thank God, he was free of being responsible for her.

In two weeks his mom would take a three-month cruise with his aunt and he would be free of what his mom called her "little problems." Since Reame was the only one of her children close by, she tended to call him. A lot. She also wasn't averse to guilting him into visiting, and when that didn't work, she made up little stories about her health or problems with her house to bring him running.

Those two weeks and freedom couldn't come soon enough. He was going to party hard and date wild women, women who knew the score, who wanted nothing more than a good time. He was going to sow all the wild oats he'd been storing up over the past ten years and he was going to sow them hard and sow them well.

The thought that he might be wanting wild because he was avoiding love and commitment jumped into his head. He was self-aware enough to realize that his quest for me-time went deeper than a simple desire to walk on the wild side. He prided himself on being responsible and part of that responsibility was not subjecting any woman to the chance that he might, like his dad, fail at a relationship, at being what a woman wanted, or needed. He'd never failed in his life and he didn't intend to start now.

Deeper reasons or not, he damn well deserved to live life hard and fast, responsible only for himself. His motivations could wait until he worked this restlessness out of his system.

Approaching the baseball center, Reame decided that he could start tonight, if he was so inclined. After he dropped Shaw off with Tate, he could go out, do something. Reame shook his head, thinking that he didn't feel like hitting a bar and spinning a line. He'd joined a dating app a few months back and maybe it was time he actually put it to its full use. New York was a big city and, in the little free time he had, he trawled through the photos, swiping right when he found someone he found attractive. He'd had a couple of quick conversations with

a few women but hadn't made any firm plans with
anyone to meet in real life.

That brown-eyed blonde was hot and there was
that psychologist who intrigued him more than most.
He tried to remember what she looked like but Lachlyn Latimore's face jumped onto the big screen of
his mind.

Dating Linc's new sister wasn't an option for a
hundred and ten reasons. *Not constructive thinking,
dude, not constructive at all.* Frustrated with himself, Reame decided to work and, as per usual, he
promised himself that in the morning he'd make it a
priority to find himself a date.

Reame pulled open the door to the baseball center
and looked down when Shaw tugged his coat. "You
really aren't listening to me, Unca Reame."

Reame winced. He hadn't heard a word Shaw had
said. "Sorry, bud, what's up?"

Shaw reached inside his jacket and Reame saw a
scaly tail, tiny feet and the pissed-off face of Spike,
Shaw's bearded dragon. "Spike's going to want pizza
when we're done. Batting makes him hungry."

Yeah, food wasn't what he was hungry for. But if
Lachlyn Ballantyne offered to eat pizza with him,
preferably naked, he was sure he could force down
a slice or two.

# Two

Back at The Den, which was situated a block or so from Central Park, Lachlyn was being guided by Linc down the hall to a set of stairs leading to a great room on the ground floor. A small picture on the wall to her left caught her eye and she sucked in a quick gasp. That couldn't possibly be a Picasso, could it? They walked past a nineteenth-century drop-leaf table, every inch of its highly polished surface covered with heavy silver frames containing photos of the current members of the Ballantyne family. Lachlyn hauled in a breath, trying to get some air to her too-tight lungs.

Up until her fifteenth birthday, being a normal girl—being part of a normal American family—had been her deepest desire, the one thing she wished for above all else. Living with an emotionally checked-out mother and an older brother who'd been forced to work to help supplement their mom's meager income, she'd grown up mostly alone. Lachlyn had comforted herself by imagining another life, cutting out pictures of wholesome, happy families from magazines and carefully pasting them into scrapbooks. She'd covered the walls of her shoebox bedroom, naming her pretend brothers and sisters and weaving fantasies about midnight snack parties, days at the beach, family arguments and Sunday lunches.

She'd made scrapbooks filled with smart and witty friends, fantasy boyfriends and carefully cut out pictures of men who looked like they'd gallop into her life and rescue her.

Then, one summer's night, her illusions about family, about the bonds that tied people together, had been shattered. Lachlyn's crash with reality had been brutal—she'd ripped the pictures from her wall, shredded her scrapbooks. What was the point, she'd decided, of living in a dream world? Lachlyn had finally accepted that she was alone, that she couldn't, and wouldn't, expect anyone—not family, not a friend, not a lover—to run to her rescue, to be there to support her when her world fell apart. She was the only person she could rely on, *would* rely on. She'd decided, then and there, not to ask, or expect, anything from anyone ever again.

She'd been young but she'd made the right choice and she still lived her life around that decision. Few friends, no boyfriends, some contact with her brother. But damn, those photos made her feel just the teeniest bit envious.

"Are you okay, Lachlyn?" Linc asked. "You look a little pale."

She wasn't used to fancy houses containing amazing artwork, she'd just met the first man who'd ever managed to set her skin on fire and she had no idea of the agenda of this upcoming meeting with the Ballantynes. Was it any surprise that she felt a little, well, stressed?

Lachlyn stopped and half turned to look at him. She wanted to say something smart or charming but she saw sympathy in his eyes. She wanted to tell him that she was feeling overwhelmed, by who the Ballantynes were and the fact that there were so many of them. But it had been a long time since Lachlyn had confided in anyone about how she was feeling. "I'm fine."

Linc's gentle smile suggested that he didn't believe her and Lachlyn realized how very good-looking he was. Actually, all the siblings looked like they could grace magazine covers and, if she wasn't mistaken, they all had at one time or the other. Sexy, educated, talented and successful, the Ballantynes were the American dream personified. Yet Lachlyn, the only person who carried Connor Ballantyne's direct DNA, was anything but.

"I understand that this is a lot to deal with, Lachlyn," Linc said, his deep voice reassuring. "For that reason, it's just us tonight, the siblings. You, me, Jaeger, Beck and Sage."

Four against one…

One meeting, a discussion, and she would be done

with them, Lachlyn thought, walking into a great room that rolled from a gourmet kitchen into a dining area and then a messy, lived-in space filled with comfortable furniture, books and toys.

Jaeger and Beck stood up and both shook her hand. Sage sent her a hesitant smile from the corner of the huge couch, her feet tucked under her bottom. Her face looked drawn and she had purple stripes under her eyes. Man trouble, Lachlyn decided. And the man causing the trouble was her brother Tyce.

Cue another awkward moment, but she couldn't ignore Sage's pain so she stopped next to Sage, bent down and touched her arm with the very tips of her fingers. "Is everything okay? The baby?"

Sage nodded and Lachlyn noticed that Sage's eyes were red-rimmed and bloodshot. "The baby is fine but your brother is driving me mad," Sage told her, trying to sound jaunty but failing miserably.

Lachlyn wanted to tell Sage that Tyce was a product of their past, of a family that had no idea how to do family. Or relationships.

"I'm sorry, Sage," Lachlyn murmured, feeling obligated to apologize. Latimores sucked at relationships in general; she needed her solitude and Tyce had his own hang-ups. She and Tyce were masters of the art of self-protection.

Jaeger waited for her to sit before handing her a glass of red wine and then resumed his seat between Sage and Beck on the big sofa. Linc sat down on the ottoman between her and Sage and took a long pull from the bottle of beer Jaeger had offered him.

"So, let's get to the heart of the matter of why you're here," Linc said.

Lachlyn placed her wine on the coffee table and clasped her hands together. Linc was going to offer her a payoff, a lump sum of money to go away, to fade into anonymity. They would buy back the Ballantyne International shares Tyce had bought for her and they would squash the reports surfacing in the press about her parentage and connection to the family.

All would go back to being normal. She couldn't wait. People exhausted her.

"We had a discussion about you, about your arrival in our life and what that meant to us," Linc said, his eyes not leaving her face. "The past year has been one of phenomenal change…six months ago we were all single. Now we have life partners."

Jaeger flashed his pirate's grin. "A hell of a lot of babies on the way. Piper, Cady, Sage…"

"Some by blood, all by love," Beck murmured. He raised an inquiring eyebrow at Linc, who instantly shook his head.

"We have a five-year-old bandit and an eighteen-month-old bandit-in-training," Linc retorted, answering the unspoken question. "We've got all we can handle at the moment."

Lachlyn shook her head, trying to keep up with their banter. She hoped pregnancy wasn't contagious. Oh, wait, you had to have sex to get pregnant. Just then the image of a pair of grape-green eyes in a tanned face appeared in her mind. Yeah, that wasn't going to happen…ever.

"It would be a manageable three but Jaeger had to be his usual obnoxious self and one up the rest of us by impregnating Piper with twin boys," Beck muttered, hooking his thick arm around Jaeger's neck and pulling it tight.

While Lachlyn enjoyed Jaeger and Beck's banter, she just wished Linc would get on with his little speech. There was more to come and Lachlyn preferred quick and nasty to kind and drawn out.

"Let's get back to why we are here," Sage suggested and Lachlyn smiled her appreciation. She'd listen, finish her wine, refuse their payoff and leave…

Linc pushed his hand through his hair. "When Tyce told us that you were Connor's daughter we were shocked, Lachlyn. Connor, as you know, died a few years ago but he suffered from Alzheimer's so even if he was alive, we couldn't ask him. But DNA doesn't lie and you *are* part of this family."

Wait, that didn't sound like a brush-off…

Linc continued. "If Connor knew about you, you would've been raised by him, of that we have no doubt. Connor was anti-marriage and commitment but he was not anti-responsibility and he adored us, kids who weren't his kids. He would've loved you."

Lachlyn wanted to ask Linc to back up, to repeat what she thought she'd heard. They considered her to be a part of this family, a Ballantyne? They wanted her to stay in the fold? *What?* She wasn't part of this family, she didn't want to be!

"And, as Connor's child, we believe it's only fair that you receive a portion of his estate."

They weren't offering to pay her off but were offering her more. Lachlyn pushed the words up her tight throat and through her bloodless lips. "A portion?"

Linc leaned forward, his forearms on his thighs and his beer bottle dangling from his fingers. "As siblings, we own many joint assets and we want to share ownership of those assets with you."

"Assets?"

Linc nodded to a file on the coffee table. "Shares, art, property, gemstones. They are all listed in there. We've also agreed to each pay you a fixed amount from our personal bank accounts to reduce the cash disparity between us."

"Uh…how much?" Lachlyn asked, her thoughts reeling.

Linc's eyes cooled and Lachlyn knew that he was disappointed by her response. It did sound grasping and gold-digger-ish but she needed to know the amount of money they were talking about, how serious they were. Ten, twenty thousand?

"We thought we'd start with ten million each but that could be negotiated."

Ten? Million? Forty million in total? Whoa…!

Lachlyn placed her head between her knees as the air in the room disappeared. She'd been expecting a brush-off, a couple of thousand to go away, and they were offering her tens of millions. Most frightening of all, they were asking her to stay. They wanted her to be a Ballantyne…

No, that wasn't possible. She didn't do people, relationships, family…

Lachlyn felt Sage perch on the arm of her chair, a small hand landing on her curved back. "Honey, are you okay?"

Lachlyn shook her head. "No," she muttered.

"You'll get used to the idea," Sage said, her hand rubbing the length of her spine. "After a while you realize that it's just money, just another tool."

Lachlyn's eyes widened and she held herself still. Oh, God, they thought that she was freaking about the money? Yeah, it was king's ransom but… so what? No, they had it all wrong. It wasn't the financial side that scared her, it was their offer to include her as a part of a family, their family. She was a loner, someone who was comfortable on her own, who liked living her life solo. She didn't do family… hell, she barely did friends!

But God, forty million dollars. How did one just dismiss that much money? Lachlyn looked inside herself and realized that she could, easily. She didn't need wealth, she needed emotional security, and keeping her distance from people, family and men, gave her what she needed.

It was a hell of a generous offer and she couldn't just toss it back in their faces. Lachlyn started to speak but Beck held up his hand.

"As you might be aware, the press has cottoned on

to your connection to us and we're predicting a lot of media attention," Beck said, looking grave. "And when I say a lot, I mean a firestorm."

Damn, just what she needed. Four sets of eyes rested on her face and Lachlyn knew that they were waiting for a reply to their offer, some sort of indication of what she was thinking. All she knew for sure was that it was all a little too much and far too soon. She didn't know them and they sure as hell didn't know her. They all needed time before some massive decisions were made that could, and would, have huge ramifications.

Lachlyn lifted her head and sat up straight. She looked each of the Ballantyne men in the eye before sending Sage the same determined look. She took a sip of her wine and stood up, begging her knees to lock. "I very much appreciate the offer but I'd like to suggest that we not make any major decisions, especially financial ones, yet."

Linc exchanged a long look with his siblings and Lachlyn sensed that she'd somehow passed a test, that their approval of her was climbing.

"I came here," Lachlyn said, sounding hesitant, "thinking that I would have a drink and then go back to my life, my very normal, solitary life. However, hearing about the impending press attention changes that. I can't ignore the impact this will have and I can't just walk away. Nor can I accept your very generous offer."

"Do you think that there's a chance that you might be able to one day?" Sage asked.

"I don't know," Lachlyn said, standing up. "I need to think. And I need to go."

Too much information, too many people. She had to leave, get out, find a quiet spot where she could make sense of this crazy turn her life had taken. Lachlyn, needing air and needing to get away, snatched up her bag and ran.

The news that Lachlyn Latimore was Connor Ballantyne's daughter had not generated the firestorm of attention Beck had predicted. It was far worse than that, Lachlyn decided. She could only describe the constant media presence as the love child of a swarm of locusts and the apocalypse. Because every word she uttered was dissected and every step she took was monitored, Lachlyn agreed to take a two-week vacation from her job as an archivist at the New York Public Library, hoping that the furor would soon subside. She also, reluctantly, agreed to move into The Den because journalists and photographers blocked both entrances to her apartment in Woodside.

To a woman who craved solitude and privacy, Lachlyn felt like she was under siege and that there was no end in sight. She was, mentally and physically, about to jump out of her skin.

It was Cady, Beck's wife and Ballantyne's PR guru who finally persuaded her that it wasn't in her interest to hide from the press—the sooner she gave them the access they wanted, the quicker the attention would die down and life would return to normal. Well, a new type of normal. Cady suggested a photo shoot, interviews with Ballantyne-friendly journalists, and a live spot on morning TV watched by—eeek!—millions, along with other magazine and print interviews.

Lachlyn said no to everything and prayed that some celebrity would do something truly shocking to draw attention away from her. Sage provided some distraction by accepting Tyce's proposal and their engagement was an excellent excuse for a ball. It was also the perfect vehicle, Cady decided, for the Ballantynes to introduce Lachlyn to their friends and business associates. And that was the only reason Lachlyn was standing in the fantastic ballroom of the iconic Forrester Hotel, dressed in an on-loan-from-Sage designer cocktail dress that cost more than she earned a year, making small talk with people who were sometimes sweet, sometimes rude, and always curious.

It was a shark tank, Lachlyn thought, taking a tiny sip of her now flat champagne. And she was the minnow trying not to be a snack.

"Are you okay?"

Lachlyn felt fingers on her elbow and turned around to see Sage. Sage glowed from the inside out, her blue eyes luminous with happiness. Her brother's declaration of love had done that, Lachlyn thought, proud of her sibling. Tyce had taken a chance on love and looked as happy as Sage did.

Brave Tyce.

Sage's inquiring eyebrow reminded her that she'd been asked a question. "I'm fine, thanks."

"Are you thoroughly sick of everyone asking the same questions?" Sage tilted her head to the side, her bright blue eyes frank.

Lachlyn pulled a face and nodded her agreement. Sage took her half-empty glass from her hand, half turned and nodded to a large ornamental lemon tree in the corner. "You look like you need a break."

"I really do," Lachlyn agreed. She was thoroughly peopled out.

"Behind that lemon tree is a small spiral staircase. It leads up to a small, secluded balcony with a great view of the ballroom. It's not big enough for any illicit shenanigans so nobody goes up there, but it's a great place to hang out for a little while and get your breath back."

Lachlyn looked up and she could see a tiny Juliet balcony, partially obscured by a wrought-iron trellis. Yes, that was exactly where she needed to be, for an hour or three. For the rest of the night if she got really, really lucky. Then Lachlyn remembered that she was one of the reasons for the ball and frowned. "Are you sure it will be okay?"

"Just go, Lachlyn, because Old Mrs. Preston is heading in your direction and she's wearing her 'I'll harangue the truth out of her' expression. I'll head her off while you make your escape."

Lachlyn flashed her a quick smile. "Thanks, Sage."

"Sure." Sage returned the smile and moved to intercept the super-thin, super-Botoxed specimen heading in her direction. Lachlyn skirted two men in tuxedos who looked like they wanted to talk to her, ignored the call for her attention and headed for the waiter standing near the hidden staircase. She picked up a fresh glass of champagne and ducked up the spiral staircase, holding her floor-length chiffon dress off the stairs. She stepped onto the small balcony and rested her back against the wall. A little peace, finally.

Needing to mentally escape, her thoughts drifted to the collection she was in the process of archiving for the New York Public Library. The grandson of a noted French art collector and critic had recently bequeathed his grandfather's entire collection of diaries, letters, art and mementoes detailing the Parisian art world of the 1920s. It was a fascinating look back into the glamorous era between the two World Wars and the project of a lifetime.

She couldn't wait for her two weeks' vacation to be over so that she could get back to work, to her quiet, empty-of-people apartment. Hearing shouts of laughter, Lachlyn looked through the trellis onto the ballroom below. She took in the exquisite gowns and breathtaking jewelry, carefully made-up faces and sophisticated conversation. A jazz band played in the corner and a few couples were on the dance floor, swaying to the 1940s ballad.

Lachlyn's eyes drifted over faces, easily finding her brother Tyce, his arms wrapped around Sage's baby bump. Tyce couldn't understand her need to hold the Ballantynes—and the world—at an arm's length. However, their agreement that she deal with the Ballantynes on her own terms was holding. Just.

Tyce didn't realize that Lachlyn was perfectly fine on her own, that he needed this amazing family, a great love affair, more than she did. She hadn't told him, or anybody, what happened that summer so long ago...

She didn't need to try hard to remember the sour smell of his breath on her face, the taste of his slimy tongue, the feel of his rough hands inside her shirt, between her legs. She'd yelled and screamed but her mom—thanks to depression, sleeping pills or, most likely, disinterest—hadn't lifted her head to help her. Before the assault had turned from horrible to devastating, Lachlyn's elbow had connected with her assailant's nose. She'd followed that up with a knee to his scrotum and he'd scuttled off. She'd sat on the floor of her bedroom, weeping and alone. As a result, asking for any type of support or help, emotional or physical, transported her back to feeling like a helpless little girl, and that was something she never wanted to be seen as. Yeah, it also stopped her from making friends, from having normal relationships with normal men, but that was a small price to pay.

Sometimes, in the early, honest hours of the morning, she suspected that she still might be that girl who didn't want to do it on her own, who might want a man, a family...that she might want to, sometimes, *lean*. What stopped her from exploring that terrifying scenario was remembering the past, the experience of looking for support—asking for help—and finding no one there.

No, she was better off alone.

Lachlyn felt the change in atmosphere and she stepped up to the trellis, trying to find the source of the disturbance. Yep, and there he was, the *alphaest* of alphas. Lachlyn took a sip of her cool champagne, enjoying the way it replaced the moisture in her mouth. She'd only met Reame Jepsen twice, the first time at The Den and she'd had another brief encounter with him at the art gallery when Tyce proposed to Sage. But despite not spending more than ten minutes in total with the blasted man, she was irritated that he was the star of some of her very sexy dreams.

Like most alpha males, Reame was big, six foot three, six four? Lachlyn's fingers curled around the trellis as she watched him move across the ballroom. Greeting someone she knew was important, Reame gripped the other man's hand, flashing a practiced smile. Mr. Important dipped his head, a clear indication that he was submitting to the alpha male. Reame stepped into the group Mr. Important was standing with, and all four men, two CEOs of Fortune 500 companies, an investment banker and a world renowned economist, took a tiny step back. Reame Jepsen dominated the space, claiming it as his own. He was the super-alpha in a room of men who were accustomed to calling the shots and taking charge.

Lachlyn released a long sigh. Reame Jepsen bothered her.

No, he bothered the hell out of her.

And here came the moths to the flame, Lachlyn thought, amused. A tall, thin blonde spun around from the next group, squealed and all but threw herself into Reame's arms. Cheeks were kissed before the blonde was elbowed out of the way by a redhead, then a brunette. She supposed it was business as usual for Reame. With his caramel-colored hair, olive skin, masculine face and light eyes, he made female eyes water, ovaries quiver and brains start to churn. Linc's best friend, or so she'd heard, was the most eligible bachelor since Connor Ballantyne, and that list had included, up until very recently, her very hot and rich brothers.

He was a catch, a prize, a goal.

Lachlyn wasn't a game-playing girl.

She was about to turn away, about to pull her eyes off his angles-and-planes face when his head shot up and their eyes clashed and held. He lifted the glass of whiskey to his lips, his light eyes not leaving her face, ignoring the woman hanging off his arm. Lachlyn stared down at him as the air between them fizzled and crackled.

She wanted him.

She was pulsing with lust, attraction, desire, need. Hot, spiky lust. Her womb was as tight as a drum and her lungs had lost their ability to breathe. Lachlyn felt the hair on the back of her neck prickle, goose bumps lifting the skin on her arms. The thought of that sexy mouth on hers, what it would feel like, how he would taste—whiskey, mint, man—drowned out rational thought. The fantasy of her dress up to her waist, his hands on the back of her thighs, her back against the wall as he slid into her was as strong as a memory from yesterday, as powerful as reality.

She understood why. He was the biggest, most powerful, highest-ranking man in the room and millions of years of biology had programmed her, and every other woman there, to want to mate with all that strength and power. Mating with him would ensure her offspring would be given the strongest chance of survival, the best genes. Her attraction to him was pure animal instinct and nothing to cause her any concern.

But Lachlyn didn't date alpha males. Hell, she didn't date at all. It would be easy to chalk it up to what happened to her so long ago, but Lachlyn refused to give that rapist-in-training that much control over her sex life.

Sex wasn't the problem, that much she knew. No, thanks to her mom's disinterest, her lack of response, her fears had taken on a different form. Lachlyn refused to ask for anything, to give up even a small measure of her independence, to make space in her life for a man, to allow herself to ask for anything, even his company.

Men liked to feel needed and Lachlyn refused to need anyone ever again. Stalemate.

Lachlyn shook her dark thoughts away, refocusing on The Alpha Male's face. She could appreciate him for what he was, a fine specimen, and her response to him was normal, natural even. Looking at him was like looking at a Botticelli painting or a Rodin sculpture…she could admire him, appreciate his masculine beauty, but unlike art, there was a personality behind it, quite a forceful one if she read him right. He was tough and strong—someone people relied on. He would expect his woman, his mate, to allow him to protect her, to shelter her, to slay her dragons.

Lachlyn had expected the person who should love her the most to help her slay a dragon once and she'd been left to do it herself. Luckily, she'd won the battle, but she'd never put herself in the position of allowing anyone to disappoint her again.

# Three

No.

Hell to the no!

Reame took a hefty sip of his whiskey, disengaged himself from the female octopus hanging off him and wished he could be rid of the panic crawling up his throat as easily. Pushing a hand through his short hair, he looked around and saw Linc across the room. Linc caught his eyes and lifted one sandy eyebrow in a silent but demanding *What the hell is wrong with you?*

Reame was pretty sure that Linc did not want to hear that he had just had the hottest video of the newbie Ballantyne playing in his head, her head tipped back, her tangerine-colored evening dress—sporting a low dipping neckline hinting at great breasts and a thigh split that made for easy access—up around her waist and the soft material flowing over his black suit as he stood between her legs, his mouth on hers, his...

*Yeah, don't go there, Jepsen, unless you want to embarrass yourself.*

He was damn sure that Linc didn't want to know any of that.

Reame ordered another whiskey from a passing waiter and glanced up to the Juliet balcony, spotting the swish of the orange dress, the flash of a pale neck. He frowned, noticing that the new Ballantyne had cut her hair, that her waist-length, platinum-blond hank of hair was gone. Dammit, he'd had fantasies about winding that hair a couple of times around his fist as he slid into her, those long strands sliding over his stomach, over his...

Reame aimed a mental roundhouse kick at his temple. Lachlyn was not a wild woman and she was not anyone he could tangle with. She was his oldest friend's new sister and you didn't fool around with your best bud's baby sister. Lachlyn was also Connor's daughter and he owed Connor so much—without him he wouldn't have his business. And he definitely didn't mess around with women with eyes that were a curious combination of lapis lazuli, vulnerability and sky-high intelligence.

Lachlyn Latimore was Trouble with a capital *T* and if he was as smart as they said he was, he'd stay far, far away from her. She wasn't what he wanted, wasn't the here now, gone tomorrow woman he was looking for.

"Stop scowling," Linc said. "You're scaring my guests."

"Wasn't."

Reame cursed silently as Linc gestured for Lachlyn to join them. Reame saw her send a quick look toward the exit, as if she were judging how quickly she could escape. Her shoulders slumped as she started to make her way toward them through the crowd, and Reame couldn't decide whether to feel insulted or to sympathize.

Linc picked up Reame's whiskey off a tray and appropriated the drink as his own. Reame tossed him a hot insult and considered wrestling the glass out of his hand. Deciding to be an adult, he jammed his hands into the pockets of his suit pants and ordered another drink. Hopefully, it would arrive soon.

"Why the frown?" Linc asked.

Reame shrugged, deliberately not meeting Linc's gaze. "You know how much I loathe these society events. I'd rather be in a firefight than here."

Linc smiled. "I know and I appreciate your sacrifice."

Reame narrowed his eyes at Linc's gentle sarcasm. Turning his back to his approaching fantasy-come-to-life, he spread his legs wide and folded his arms across his chest. He studied Linc and saw the worry in his eyes, the tense muscle in his jaw. "What do you need, bro?"

Before he could reply, Lachlyn stepped up to Linc's side and sent Reame a cool look. "Hello, Reame."

"Lachlyn," Reame replied with equal ice. Look at them, he thought, pretending that they hadn't just imagined each other naked and writhing five minutes earlier. "You look nice."

If nice meant sensationally and spectacularly sexy.

Those blues darkened to violet as a blush crossed her cheeks. "Thank you."

"Linc was just about to ask me something..." Reame turned back to Linc who tossed back the rest of his whiskey and then rolled the glass between the palms of his hands. Keeping his voice low so that he wasn't overheard, Linc answered his question. "The reaction to the news that Lachlyn is a Ballantyne and that we have accepted her into the fold has been bigger and more intense than any of us, including Cady, expected. Lachlyn has moved into The Den, Reame, and for the last few days the press have camped on the sidewalk. None of us can get in and out of the house without being harassed. Lachlyn tried to go out yesterday and they nearly ripped her apart. She ran into the house looking like the hounds of hell were on her tail."

"I think that's a bit of an exaggeration," Lachlyn interjected.

"Shh." Reame hushed her, wanting Linc to continue. Before he could, Linc was distracted by an old lady with diamonds the size of quail eggs and wrinkles as deep as the Mariana Trench.

Linc turned his attention to the Grand dame and Lachlyn took the opportunity to launch her small elbow into his side. "Don't you shush me!" she hissed.

"I wanted to hear what Linc was saying and you were interrupting him," Reame replied, willing her eyes to flash violet again. "Maybe kissing you to shut you up would've worked better. Far more enjoyable…"

Yep, violet, with sparks of silver. "Are you drunk?"

Drunk on… *Do not even complete that thought, Jepsen.* What the hell is wrong with you? Reame's thumb found the pulse point on her inside wrist and, yep, there it was, her heart beating as fast as a hummingbird's wing. His wasn't far behind. He glanced at Linc, made sure he wasn't listening before speaking. "I know that you were imagining us naked."

Reame just managed to stop himself from lifting her hand to kiss the delicate skin under his fingers.

Lachlyn jerked her hand away. "Your illusions are insulting and annoying. And I need a drink."

He could relate. "Bring me one? A double whiskey on the rocks?" Reame asked, his tone teasing. He wasn't surprised when she rolled her eyes and flounced away from him, her compact and curvy body radiating annoyance.

Reame sighed. Not the way to make friends with the new Ballantyne…

But, dammit, even before he'd met her, she'd *bothered* him. Bother was now too small a word to use to describe how she made him feel…

And why—when there were at least thirty women here whom he could hit on, if he excluded the married ones and he so did—was he wanting to get up close, very close and very naked, with *her*? With his best friend's new sister?

Screwed, he decided. If he didn't get a grip he would be so screwed.

Reame lifted his eyebrows when Linc turned back to him having given the Lady of the Big Diamonds sufficient attention. "You were saying…"

Linc pushed a hand through his blond hair. "Someone dug up Lachlyn's phone number and her phone has been ringing off the hook. She's being harassed on social media and it doesn't look to be dying down anytime soon."

Reame nodded his understanding. "I'll get my cyber guy to bury her social security number, to take her off the Net as much as possible. He'll change her address to your box number and get her a new phone number under one of my companies. We'll put firewalls around her social media accounts. You know the drill."

Linc should. He and his guys had done the same thing for Connor and all the Ballantynes after him. High-profile families attracted criminals and nutcases, and sometimes the nutcases were criminals, too.

Reame waited, knowing that there was more. Linc scratched his chin, his eyes flat with worry. "Tate has to film in the Rockies this coming week and I was planning on joining her there with the kids."

Somehow, Linc and Tate managed to combine his hectic and pressurized job as Ballantyne CEO with

Tate's job as a travel presenter without neglecting Shaw or Ellie, their adopted daughter.

"I don't want to leave Lachlyn in The Den by herself but she adamantly refuses to move in with Sage and Tyce or with Jaeger or Beck."

Since she'd be the third wheel wherever she went—all the Ballantynes were still in the cooing and billing stage of their relationship—Reame didn't blame her.

"What's her apartment like?" Reame asked.

"Small, I imagine," Linc said.

"Would it be feasible for one of my female personal protection people to move in with her?" Reame asked.

"I don't think so but what do I know? Lachlyn doesn't talk!"

Reame knew that Lachlyn still hadn't accepted their offer to become a full Ballantyne partner but in the eyes of the world she was assumed to be a very wealthy woman. As such, she was a target. Linc was right, she needed a bodyguard and to live in a place with excellent security.

And security was his business. "How does she feel about having security?"

Linc pulled a face. "She thinks I'm overreacting. She has this idea that she'll be able to go back to work next week, that the furor will have died down by then. She's dreaming if she thinks a haircut will make her look less recognizable." Linc lifted his chin in Lachlyn's direction and Reame finally, finally had an excuse to look at her again.

As he'd noticed earlier, her hair was now short and choppy. Her bangs twisted away from her face, revealing high cheekbones, those incredible sin-with me eyes, her made-to-be-kissed (but not by him) lips. Despite her two-inch heels, she still only reached his shoulder, and without her stilts she barely scraped five-two. Her body, despite her being a fairy, was all woman. Full and perky breasts, a waist he could span with his hands, long legs and round hips.

And a truly excellent ass.

"She needs protection, Ree."

Reame groaned, wondering whom he had to kill to get another drink. He ignored the action in his pants and focused on business, on what Linc was asking him to do. He swallowed his sigh. If it was anyone else but Linc making the request, he'd decline the business. He didn't have enough staff to meet the demand for personal protection officers as it was. Liam, his head of operations, was going to kill him. And Liam, being ex-military, as well, actually could follow up on his threat.

But this was Linc asking… "Let me call around tomorrow and have a chat with her, and you. What time are you leaving?"

"Midmorning," Linc replied, briefly grasping Reame's bicep in a show of his appreciation. "Thanks, bud. Will you please charge me or the firm? God knows we can afford it."

Reame shook his head and, as he always did, ignored Linc's request. After he left the military, Connor gave him his first job, had recommended him to his rich friends and clients and he'd lent him the capital to start up his security business. Together with Linc, Connor had been his biggest supporter and his best advertiser, and it was because of their support and loyalty that his company was now regarded to be the best in the city. His business had put his three sisters through college, paid for the fancy apartment he lived in, the repairs on his mom's house. It employed many of his ex-army buddies and sent ridiculous amounts of money into his personal bank account.

For as long as he owned Jepsen & Associates, he would swallow any costs the Ballantynes' personal security needs generated.

He owed Linc, his brothers and Connor a debt he couldn't repay but he'd sure as hell try. Because, unlike his father, he believed in loyalty and responsibility.

He looked at life straight on, readily accepting that it was a series of waves and troughs, shallow waters and depths. All one could do was just keep swimming.

Reame looked across the room at Lachlyn and studied her exquisite profile, the horrible thought occurring to him that she might be the one woman who could make him drown.

The next morning, Lachlyn glanced down at the screen of her phone, thinking it was another call from a super-pushy reporter, but instead she saw the familiar number of her supervisor at the New York Public Library. Annie was not only her direct boss but the closest person she had to an older sister and best friend.

"Hey, hun, how are you holding up?" Annie asked as Lachlyn placed her flat palm against the cool window of the small upstairs living room of The Den.

"Fair to horrible," Lachlyn said, pulling the drape aside to look down at the sidewalk. The crowd standing behind the wrought-iron fence was talking amongst themselves, although many cameras were pointed toward the front door. Somebody caught her movement and, almost immediately, a dozen cameras lifted in her direction. Lachlyn abruptly stepped back and ignored the muted roars for a comment, a photo opportunity, an interview. Rubbing her forehead, she slid down the wall until an expensive Persian carpet was all that separated her denim-covered butt from the rich wooden floors. "I can't wait to come back to work next week."

There was a long pause and Lachlyn's stomach jumped. Annie was usually incredibly voluble and she didn't do silence. "That's not going to happen anytime soon, Lach."

Lachlyn felt her headache intensify. "What do you mean?"

"There's too much attention around you, on you. The phones have been ringing off the hook, people asking anyone and everyone for information on you. It's mayhem, Lach, and you aren't even here."

The monster chomping its way through her stomach took another huge bite. "What exactly are you saying, Annie?"

"My supervisor is suggesting that you take all of your vacation time. It adds up to about two months." Annie said in a tone that suggested she'd been practicing how to break the news.

"I don't have a job anymore?" Lachlyn whispered, terrified that what she was hearing was her new reality.

"You don't have a job for the next few months. After that, we'll see," Annie said, trying to sound jaunty. "Since, according to the press, money is no longer an object, you could tour the great libraries of the world, visit the museums you always talk about going to, see the amazing art you look at in books," Annie said, her voice turning persuasive. "This is an opportunity, Lach, not a punishment."

But Annie didn't understand that, while she didn't mind being alone, she hated not being busy, not having a purpose. Having nothing to do reminded her of her childhood, of long days and nights without company or conversation, with only an old television set for entertainment. Her mother would come home from work, pop some sleeping tabs she bought from the guy on the corner and pass out for the next fourteen or sixteen hours. Tyce was always out, selling his art in the park so that they could pay one of the many bills her mom couldn't cover. The local library had been her favorite place to hang out and books her constant and unfailing friends. These days she spent most of her time alone but her work kept her busy.

"Lachlyn? Lachlyn?"

Lachlyn forced herself to blink, concentrating on

the cool floor beneath her hand, allowing the noise from the photographers to drift up to her. Then she saw that the display screen on her phone still showed that she was connected to Annie.

"I've got to go, Annie."

"Look," Annie said, "if your situation changes I can have another talk with Martin." But Lachlyn heard her underlying frustration, her *Why would you want to spend your days digging through old papers when you could be shopping and seeing the world, playing the role of the Park Avenue Princess?*

Nobody realized that accepting the money was the easy part. It was just a couple more zeroes—okay, a lot more zeroes—in her bank account. She could take it or leave it, spend it or give it away. It was the people involved that made this difficult, the fact that this wasn't just a matter of moving cash around. The family dynamic of who and what the Ballantynes were and stood for made this situation complicated. A cold hand squeezed her lungs together and she deliberately slowed her breathing down and released her grip on her phone, shaking her hand to put blood back into her fingers. A few months earlier, when Tyce had told her that he was making plans for her to meet her biological family she'd thought that she'd meet the Ballantynes, have a meal with them and that they'd all go back to their very different lives.

She never expected to be offered a fat bank account, a limitless credit card, to be moved into The Den and to be hounded by the press. The possibility of being accepted as part of the family never crossed her mind. She was touched by their actions, amazed at their generosity but underneath it all, she was running scared, bone-deep terrified. Beneath the fame and money, the Ballantynes were people, and people meant relationships.

She didn't do relationships… How could she make them see that?

"Lachlyn?"

Lachlyn heard Reame's low, deep voice and scrambled to her feet. She ducked her head and dashed her fingers against her cheeks, annoyed when she wiped away moisture. The last thing she needed was Reame to see her tears.

Lachlyn looked at the now empty doorway, looking for Linc. His presence would, hopefully, stop her from making an ass of herself with his best friend.

"Hi." Lachlyn placed her shaking hands into the back pockets of her jeans and felt a hole in the corner of one of the pockets. She was wearing ragged jeans, a long-sleeve white T-shirt and banged-up sneakers, while Reame looked fantastic in his dark jeans, pale blue shirt and cream jacket. The royal blue pocket square was a nice touch. He pulled designer shades off the top of his head and tapped the glasses against his empty palm.

Reame managed a tight smile and his eyes skittered off hers. Huh. "Where's Linc?" she asked, darting a hopeful look at the door he'd closed behind him.

"Shaw."

Reame didn't have to say any more; in the few

days that she'd spent in The Den, there had been a few "Shaw" moments.

"Ah, enough said," Lachlyn said, rocking on her heels.

Reame walked over to the window and, standing to the side, pulled back the drape so that he could see out without being photographed. "The crowd looks bigger than it was twenty minutes ago."

"I just wish they would go away," Lachlyn muttered. "I don't understand why they are so interested in me."

"You're young, pretty and you've just won the family jackpot. You are news," Reame said in a flat voice, his back still to her. "You're a modern-day fairy tale playing out in front of their eyes."

Reame turned around and gestured to the comfortable couch. "Take a seat. It's a lot more comfortable than the floor."

Since he noticed she'd been sitting on the cold floor, Lachlyn knew that there was no chance that he'd missed her red-rimmed eyes and her wobbly lip. Reame Jepsen, Lachlyn suspected, didn't miss a damn thing.

Pride had her forcing her shoulders back, lifting her chin as she made her way to the couch and perched on the edge of the cushion.

Reame sat opposite her and leaned forward, his forearms resting on his legs, his hands dangling between his strong thighs. This morning, his eyes were a cool, light peppermint and, as always, invasive. She felt like he could see into her soul, read her thoughts.

Lachlyn felt exposed and uncomfortable. God, she hoped that this conversation wouldn't take long.

"Let's talk security, specifically your security," Reame said, his eyes cool and tone brusque.

Lachlyn forced herself to maintain eye contact and responded with a nod.

"Linc is concerned about you being on your own."

"He doesn't need to be. I'm used to being on my own."

"If you were the ordinary woman you were a month ago, I'd agree."

"But you're not Lachlyn Latimore anymore, you're now a Ballantyne—at least in the eyes of the press—and that changes the picture," Reame continued, the warm waves of his voice rolling over her skin. "You're the newest member of a very prominent, very interesting family. The residents of this city have grown up with the Ballantynes. They remember when Connor took in three orphans. They cheered when Connor adopted Linc alongside Jaeger, Beck and Sage. They mourned Connor's death. The interest in the Ballantynes has never wavered and the fact that you are Connor's daughter is big news. The Ballantynes pulling you into the family and sharing Connor's wealth with you is *huge* news."

"I'm not taking the money," Lachlyn blurted out. For some reason she couldn't articulate, it was important that he understand that she wasn't a gold digger and that she had little interest in the Ballantyne fortune.

"You're not?"

Lachlyn squeezed her hands between her thighs. "No."

Lachlyn thought she caught a flash of surprise on his face but a second later his expression turned inscrutable. Linc lifted a big shoulder in a *don't care* shrug. "That's between you and them. I'm just here to talk about keeping you safe."

Nothing in his body language, voice or eyes suggested that they'd shared a hot look across a crowded ballroom and that electricity had sizzled and sparked between them. He was all business, only business.

Good. Then why did she feel a tiny bit disappointed?

Linc sat up straight, leaned back and placed his ankle on his opposite knee. He tapped his finger on his thigh. "Linc also wants me to give you a PPO—"

That didn't sound very nice. "A what?"

"A personal protection officer, a bodyguard," he explained, sounding impatient. "You need a shield between you and the press. And any crazies."

"Crazies?"

"There are eight million people in this city, most of whom have heard or read about you. More than a few are delusional and a handful might think of you as their new best friend, as a potential lover or something more sinister. Until the attention dies down, it's wise to take precautions."

Lachlyn tried to assimilate the barrage of information, to make sense of what he was saying. It didn't help that every time she looked at him, she wondered what his lips would feel like on hers, whether his hands would be rough or smooth against her bare skin. God, she'd never looked at a man and felt her saliva dry up, her heart bang against her chest.

What was it about him that yanked her libido out of its coma?

Let's think about that… Did it have anything to do with the fact that he was the sexiest man she'd met? Ever?

Frustrated with herself, frustrated in general, Lachlyn refocused. What were they discussing? Right, bodyguards.

Reame played with the laces on his trendy shoes. "So in order to give you the best protection, I need some information about you. Let's start with the easy stuff, your job. You're a librarian?"

Lachlyn shook her head. "I work as an archivist at the NYPL."

A small smile touched Reame's mouth and a butterfly in her stomach took flight, followed by another ten. "I love that building."

The Beaux Arts building was her favorite place in the world. "I do, too."

Reame kept his eyes locked on hers, penetrating and steady. "And do you like your work?"

"I love it. Libraries, books…documents make me hot."

Reame's eyes heated and turned speculative and Lachlyn cursed her choice of words. She'd opened the door and flat-out desire walked in and plonked itself between them, its smile mocking. "Uh… I…" Lachlyn stuttered.

Reame looked away from her and Lachlyn saw his chest rise and fall as he took a big breath. His expression was so inscrutable that she couldn't tell if he was feeling the attraction too or whether he was just making an attempt to hide his irritation. So far, she'd seen nothing of the heat she'd seen in his eyes last night…maybe she'd just projected her attraction onto him. Because she was an emotional hermit, she was inexperienced with men so it was entirely possible.

"Let's talk about your living arrangements. You live in Woodside?" Reame asked, smoothly changing the subject and ignoring her flaming face. God, she had all the poise and grace of a walrus.

Lachlyn thought about her bright, cheerful space packed full of books and sighed. "I live in a small apartment above a bakery."

"And that's where you would like to be?" Reame asked.

Lachlyn darted him a hopeful look. "Oh, God, yes! But Linc seems to think that's not a good idea, that it's too small and too far away."

Reame didn't look too concerned. "I'm in the business of making life easier for my clients, not my staff. My paramount concern is your safety." In that statement Lachlyn saw the hard businessman, the tough commanding officer. She had no doubt that when Reame said hop, his people asked how far they should jump.

"If your apartment is a safe place for you to stay, then you can. If it's not, we go to plan B."

"Which is?"

"No idea. Yet." Reame said. "You will have two PPOs assigned to you. One will take the night shift and will drive you to work in the morning. I'm presuming that you aren't in the public eye at work?"

Lachlyn shook her head. "The public doesn't have access to my work area but that's not going to be an issue." Lachlyn rubbed her forehead with the tips of her fingers and shook her head. "I don't currently have a job."

Reame frowned. "They fired you?"

"No, I have a lot of vacation time, nearly two months accumulated, which I'm being ordered to take. They believe that my presence at work will be too disruptive."

"I can't disagree with that," Reame admitted. "So how are you going to fill your time?"

"I have no idea," Lachlyn said wearily. The realization was terrifying.

Lachlyn heard the discreet beep of a cell phone. Reame pulled his phone from the inside pocket of his jacket and scowled down at the screen. "I need to get back to work. The Den is one of the safest houses in the city so you will stay here for now. Later this afternoon I'll bring your PPOs around to meet you. They will escort you back to your place and take over your protection."

Reame hit the buttons on his phone and held the device to his ear. Standing up, he jammed his free hand into the front pocket of his jeans and rocked on his heels. "Cora? Reame."

Lachlyn heard the muted squawk of a female voice and thought about moving across the room to give him some privacy. Then again, he was already standing; if he wanted to move away, he could.

"Yeah, sorry, I've wasted a load of time this morning. Tell them that I will be there in twenty," Reame stated. "I need Liam to pull the folders of anyone who is available for a protection gig starting this afternoon."

Lachlyn narrowed her eyes at his wasted time comment.

"Yeah, open a file, Lachlyn Latimore… Yeah, same deal as usual."

This time the squawk was louder and Lachlyn heard the words *pro bono* and *charity*. She rocketed to her feet and held up her hands in a "just stop!" gesture. She'd been at the receiving end of too much charity in her life—clothes, food, education and she was damned if she'd take it from Reame Jepsen. Receiving something for nothing was the equivalent of asking for help and she didn't need any, especially not from him.

"No! Not pro bono and not charity," she firmly stated, interrupting the conversation. She met Reame's light eyes and forced herself not to back down at his scowling face. He dropped his phone and held it against his thigh.

"This conversation has nothing to do with you."

"The hell it doesn't," Lachlyn retorted.

Biting the edge of her thumb, she rocked on her heels. "Look, just forget the protection, I'll be fine."

"The hell you will. There are factors to this that you don't understand. Linc and I have an understanding…"

"And I'm telling you that if I can't pay, then this doesn't happen. I'll take my chances," Lachlyn told him, her scowl rivaling his.

She'd never stared down a big, burly former Special Forces soldier before and Lachlyn thought that she'd won the battle when he lifted his phone to his ear again. But Reame didn't look away. His determined expression didn't change. "Cora, two people, their folders on my desk when I get back. Open the file…pro bono."

Lachlyn narrowed her eyes at him as he disconnected the call and before she could blast him, he spoke. "My business, my rules. You don't get to comment on it."

Lachlyn pointed to herself. "My body, my protection, I pay for it."

Reame groaned. "Oh, God, you are going to be one of the pain in the ass clients aren't you?"

"Damn right I am," Lachlyn retorted, noticing his gaze jumping from her eyes to her mouth and back up again. That damn buzz passed from him to her and ignited the flames low in her belly, sending heat to her most feminine parts, the parts that craved him and his touch.

"When I get back to the office, you will officially

become a client," Reame said in a husky voice. "But you're not my client… Yet."

His words made no sense but she did notice that he was looking at her like she was a novel he'd been waiting months to read, like the latest creation by his favorite artist. Like she was a world he couldn't wait to explore. Oh, God, he looked like he wanted to kiss her.

Reame's hands shot out and gripped her hips. He yanked her closer and her stomach slammed into his body. She felt his heat and, wow, something that was long and hard and…

"I never put my hands on a client." Reame lifted his wrist and looked at his watch. "But I have some time…"

Her head whirling, Lachlyn blinked as he locked his arms around her waist, his mouth falling toward hers. Lachlyn sucked in some air—she figured she was going to need it—and felt his knees bend as he easily lifted her so that her mouth aligned with his and then… *God and heaven.*

Teeth scraped and lips soothed, tongues swirled and whirled and heat, lazy heat, spread through her limbs and slid into her veins. Reame was kissing her and time and space shifted. It felt natural for her legs to wind around his waist, to lock her arms around his neck and take what she'd been fantasizing about. Kissing Reame was better than she imagined—she was finally feeling all those fuzzy feels romance books described. For the first time ever, she felt dizzy, the butterflies in her stomach were doing complicated aerial displays and electricity river-danced on her skin.

It felt perfect. It felt right.

Reame jerked his mouth off hers and their eyes connected, his eyes now darker, intense, blazing with hot, green fire. He cursed once before diving in again. This time he didn't hesitate, didn't mess around... This was serious kissing, kissing on steroids. This was the kiss you gave a woman when you knew you could never do it again.

For the first time she could remember, her brain switched off and allowed her to live in the moment, free to taste and explore, to experience. Lachlyn pressed herself closer, she'd climb inside him if she could, and pushed her fingers into his soft hair, her other hand exploring his stubble-covered masculine jaw, his strong neck. She groaned into his mouth when his hand ducked under the hem of her loose shirt, skated beneath the band of her jeans and under the thin cord of her thong. She wanted more, his mouth on other places, his fingers dancing over all the neglected places on her body.

She wanted him... She never wanted anybody. And never this much.

"Holy crap—"

Reame stiffened in her arms and Lachlyn yanked her mouth off Reame's and looked over his shoulder to the now open door to where Linc stood, half in and half out of the room. Lachlyn slid down Reame's hard body. She pushed her bangs off her forehead and released a deep breath, grateful that Reame's big body shielded her from Linc.

Lachlyn touched her swollen lips and glanced down at her chest, where her hard nipples pushed against the fabric of her lacy bra and thin T-shirt. She couldn't possibly look more turned on if she tried. It was a very strange and confusing sensation.

"Oh, this is just perfect," Linc said. Lachlyn couldn't look at him but he sounded thoroughly amused. "Want me to go away and come back in fifteen?"

Reame looked at her and, along with desire, she thought she saw regret in his eyes. He slowly shook his head. "No, we're done."

Lachlyn met his eyes and nodded her agreement. Yes, they were done. They had to be.

# Four

Back in his office, Reame tossed his jacket over the back of his visitor's chair and threw his phone across his desk where it bounced off a photo of his mom and three sisters. He gripped the back of the chair and closed his eyes, the image of Linc's amused and speculative face bouncing around his brain. He knew that Linc had taken two plus two and reached seventy-eight million…

He knew exactly what Linc was remembering. When he left the military, Sage was in her early twenties and Connor, bless his soul, had decided to play matchmaker. Before Alzheimer's had ravaged his mind, he'd made a concerted effort to throw him and Sage together, dropping broad hints that he'd love to have Reame as a son-in-law.

There was only one problem with Connor's little fantasy: even with a gallon of gas and a flame thrower, he and Sage couldn't generate a spark.

Unlike the raging lightning storm that happened when he kissed Lachlyn. And Linc had seen it…

Reame resisted the urge to reach for his phone to dial Linc, to insist that it was only a kiss, that it didn't mean anything. That Linc should cool his jets, this wasn't going anywhere, ever. It had been a moment in time, an aberration, a curiosity. That there wasn't a chance in hell that he'd ever get involved with or marry a member of the Ballantyne family. He didn't want to marry anyone, he wanted to have a good time, to sow those wild oats that being the family breadwinner and his military career denied him. He wanted to have wild sex with wild women…

He'd recently watched his best friends—Linc and Jaeger and Beck—fall in love and assume a heavy mantle of responsibility and accountability. While he'd had a few affairs, he'd never experienced anything close to the passionate and intense situations his friends were in. Seeing them fall had just strengthened his resolve to have some fun. Relationships, anything from dating to marriage, required a degree of responsibility, and he'd been responsible enough for ten lifetimes. And there was the emotional component to consider. He'd witnessed his mom's devastation when his dad walked out on her after twenty-five years together. Who in their right mind wanted to risk that happening to them?

And worse, what if he met and married someone and then, like his dad, realized that he'd made an awful mistake? Marriage to anyone was a huge leap and marrying into the Ballantyne family was the biggest leap of all. He had a lifetime of memories tied up with them, he owed them so much and they were as much his family as his blood relatives were. If he married and messed up, it would be bad. If he married a Ballantyne and messed up, the consequences would be tragic. He'd lose his best friends, his valuable clients and a huge, wonderful part of his life. Failing at marriage was a risk he wasn't prepared to take…

But hell, that kiss had been hotter and wilder than any he could remember in recent memory.

*Crap. Hell. Dammit.*

"Reame?"

Reame whipped around and glared at his PA. "What?"

Cora fisted a hand on one ample hip and her scowl suggested that he tone down the attitude. Knowing that his life would be a lot more difficult without the super-efficient Cora in it, he reined in his temper. "Sorry, it's been a long morning and it's not even ten thirty yet."

Cora just lifted one eyebrow and stepped up to him, handing him a stack of folders. She tapped her bottom lip. "Nice shade of lip gloss you're wearing, boss."

Reame cursed and rubbed the back of his hand across his lips. Yeah, Cora on his case was exactly what he didn't need. "Do not say one damn word."

Cora folded her arms and looked up at the ceiling. "She's a client and I thought that we didn't smooch, or do anything else with, our clients. I thought that was an unbreakable rule," she teased, a smile on her lips.

*God.* "Let's try something new," Reame suggested. "Let's pretend that I am the boss, that you respect me and that I pay your salary at the end of the month."

Cora rolled her eyes. "Okay, so those are the folders of the men who are available to work with Lachlyn Latimore."

Reame, his head pounding, walked around his desk and dropped into his leather chair. He flipped open the first file, saw who it was and tossed it to one side. "Too inexperienced."

He quickly ran through the other folders, finding fault with each of the six candidates, conscious of Cora perching on the arm of his visitor's chair. He was looking over the second to last folder when a rap on his door frame had him looking up to see Daniel, one of his newest and best hires, standing in the doorway. He was also supposed to be providing security to a visiting Arab sheikh.

"Boss, I just got in and Liam said to tell you that I'm available to work tonight."

Reame frowned. "Where's the sheikh?"

"On his way back to Saudi a week early. He had a family emergency." Daniel opened his hands. "I'm free."

Nearly nine years younger than him, Daniel was twenty-six, and handsome and cocky. And he was also, damn him, charming. He was the perfect type of guy to guard Lachlyn, easygoing but professional.

Best of all, he seemed to have a sixth sense about people and could spot trouble before it even happened.

Reame opened his mouth to tell him about his new gig and the words clogged up in his throat. He couldn't get them out.

"Boss?" Daniel frowned, stepping into the room. "Are you okay?"

Cora, the witch, just smiled and waved Daniel back. "He's fine. He's just having a Damascus moment."

Daniel looked puzzled. "What does that mean?"

Cora tilted her head, her eyes on Reame's face. "Oh, just that the boss man is realizing exactly how personal this new gig is."

Reame felt irritation burn the back of his throat. He dismissed Daniel and told him to shut the door. When he was alone, he nailed Cora with a don't-mess-with-me look. "What the hell does that mean?" he demanded.

Cora didn't look even a little bit intimidated. "It means that you are not going to allow anyone to protect Lachlyn Latimore-Ballantyne but yourself."

"The hell I'm not." Reame slammed his hand on the pile of folders. "I just need half a chance to decide who will fit her best." Reaching for the handset of his desk phone, he jabbed the extension number and waited for Liam to answer. He and Liam had served together in the sandpits of the world and he was his second in charge at Jepsen Securities. After Linc, he was the man Reame trusted most.

"Daniel says that you are having some sort of moment. What the hell does that mean?"

Didn't anyone bother with a hello anymore?

Reame opened his mouth to curse him, realized that Cora was still standing there and sighed. "I need two female PPOs this afternoon for the next few weeks."

"Yeah...no," Liam replied, amused. "Have you lost your mind?"

"Possibly," Reame admitted.

"Firstly, we do not have enough woman PPOs to handle the amount of jobs we do have, and as fast as we are hiring them, the more clients we have for them. Are you asking me to pull two agents from the field for a pro bono gig?"

When Liam put it like that...

"I could, maybe, reassign Fiona, in two weeks or so," Liam said.

Yeah, too little too late. Reame banged his handset down and drummed his fingers on the surface of his desk. He picked up a file and flipped it open again. He was being ridiculous. He'd made this decision a thousand times before for hundreds of clients. Take one client, assign an agent...

Cora snorted, her expression challenging. "You can't do it, can you?"

Reame tried, again, to verbalize a name who would act as Lachlyn's PPO. Yet again, the words refused to come. Nobody, he finally admitted, was guarding Lachlyn but himself. He could rationalize his decision. She was a Ballantyne, Linc's brand-new sister. He only had his business because of Connor, so he owed it to him to give Lachlyn his undivided attention.

He was also exceptionally good at BS-ing himself.

"Shall I tell Daniel he's got the job?" Cora asked, her tone sweet but her eyes dancing with mischief. There was no way a cocky, charming stud ten years younger than him was going to spend hours alone with Lachlyn.

Cora laughed. "I thought so."

"I hate you so much right now," Reame muttered before banging his forehead on his desk.

Cora's hand patted his shoulder. "Being right never gets old. You want some coffee?"

"Yes. And I need a brain transplant. And a new PA, if you could manage that," Reame added sarcastically.

"Well, one out of three ain't bad."

Back at The Den, Lachlyn sat on one of the leather sofas in the great room and stared out of the floor-to-ceiling windows onto the postage stamp garden beyond the glass. Still feeling a little dazed, she lifted her fingertips to her lips and swore that she could taste Reame. His smell, a dizzying combination of laundry detergent, alpha male and soap, still lingered in her nose.

Lachlyn rested her elbows on her knees and cupped her face in her hands. So, wow. Wow, wow, *wow*.

In her effort to reclaim her sexuality, Lachlyn

had, when she was younger, kissed a few men, had
indulged in some heavy petting and had been taken
over the edge once or twice. Those early dates had
been hard work; fear had been her chaperone every
time. Surprisingly, it hadn't been the physicality of
the dates that had scared her. Lachlyn found that if
she liked the guys enough, she could enjoy a man's
touch and she was fine with physical intimacy.

No, what made her chest tighten and her throat
close was the emotional component. Somehow, despite her intentions to keep things casual, she always
managed to date men who wanted *more*. All of them,
within a short space of time, started talking about
taking their relationship to the next level, sleeping
over, moving in, making a deeper connection. Even
the dreaded L word had been uttered—causing her
to run as hard and fast as she could, leaving them
confused and hurt.

Over the past few years, she hadn't met many men
who could compete with a cup of tea and a great
book, so she hadn't dated much. There had been a
couple of dinners with a historian at NYU and an artist she met through Tyce. She'd controlled the pace of
the relationships. Coffee meant a light kiss, dinner,
a longer kiss. More dinners, maybe some heavy petting. Both men had wanted more—sex and a deeper
connection—so she'd let them down gently.

Kissing Reame hadn't involved any thought. She'd
just dived headfirst into that whirlpool. She'd wanted
so she took. His mouth had made her skin tingle and
her mind swim. She'd felt dazed and drunk…hell,

she still did. She still wanted more. More kisses, more skin, him completing her, making her whole. Kissing Reame had been wonderful, exciting, dizzying...

A wonderful, exciting, dizzying *mistake*.

Lachlyn stood and walked over to the door, placing her hand on the cold glass. Her libido couldn't have chosen a more inconvenient time to wake up and shake its tail. Oh, a part of her reveled in the fact that she could feel so much passion, that she was capable of more than anemic kisses and fumbling caresses. But she was neck-deep in a situation that was rapidly spinning out of control. She was dealing with the Ballantynes, was suddenly a mini-celebrity and had to make decisions that involved millions and millions of dollars.

At this crucial time in her life, at this watershed moment, she could not afford to go off tangent and explore this wonderful new world of carnal pleasure. She had bigger worries...

She had to manage the Ballantynes' expectations of her and somehow make them realize, without explaining why, that someday soon she'd be bowing out and that she wouldn't be much more than an occasional extra body at family events she was expected to attend as Tyce's sister and his baby's aunt. She couldn't explain that she was used to being on her own, that it was far easier to stand alone and that she would never need, want or ask for anything from them.

Those were her big worries, but she had others.

How was she going to fill the hours in the day without a job to go to? How was she going to cope with having a bodyguard in her face 24/7? She liked her privacy and her solitude. She didn't have a spare room and living with a stranger was shaping up to be a nightmare.

And the world thought she was living a fairy tale. Ha!

On the bright side, at least Reame wouldn't be around so she had a shot at thinking clearly and acting like an adult.

That shot was blown out of the water when Reame stepped into the hallway of The Den an hour later than he said he'd be. Lachlyn started to peek outside the front door of the famous brownstone, remembered why that wasn't a good idea and jerked her head back.

"Stand away from the door, Lachlyn," Reame said, his tone curt.

Reame closed the door with more force than necessary and pushed his jacket back to place his hands on his narrow hips. Lachlyn wondered if he had those defined hip muscles that made women swallow their tongues.

This! This was why she shouldn't be anywhere near him! "Where are my bodyguards?" she asked, finally remembering why he was back. Why was she asking about the one thing she didn't want and couldn't afford?

Reame shoved his hand through his caramel-colored hair and jerked his head at the door. "I'm it," he said, looking miserable.

Lachlyn frowned. "You're what?"

"Your security detail," Reame said, his jaw tight. "Are you ready to go?"

Frowning, Lachlyn stepped back, her hands raised. "Whoa, slow down there. What does that mean?"

"For the foreseeable future, I'm going to be the one on your six."

"On your six? What does that mean?"

Reame picked up a small bronze statue off the polished drop leaf table, tracing the delicate curves of the ballerina with his big hands. Lachlyn could almost imagine his hands on her back, stroking, kneading, exploring. She wanted that, she wanted him, but he wasn't a good idea. Hadn't she decided that a little earlier? Ten minutes with him and she was being led into temptation again.

"It means that I've got your back," Reame replied and she had to work hard to keep up with the conversation. "Whether you like it or not, I'm going to be close by."

She didn't like it, not in any shape or form. But why, if she was so opposed to the idea, did she feel a flicker of excitement at the thought of spending more time with this man?

"You can't look after me day and night," Lachlyn told him, using her hell-no voice.

"You'd think that but apparently, because I am a moron of magnificent proportions, that's what's going to happen," Reame retorted, picking up her heavy suitcase and holding it as if it were a handbag. "Look, I'm still trying to juggle some staff around to find someone who would be a suitable PPO for you. I just need a little time," Reame stated in a flat voice. "I thought that I would drive you to Woodside and check out your apartment. Once I do that, I can make better decisions about your security."

Lachlyn wrinkled her nose. "So, I might not be able to stay there tonight?" Her bed, her pillow, her things... All she wanted to do was be in a space that was hers, where she felt comfortable. But something bizarre was happening between them and there was too much heat. Her apartment was small and they'd bump into each other and boom! They'd set the place on fire.

"I'd just like to state, for the record, that you being my bodyguard is not going to work for me," Lachlyn replied, panic coating her throat and words. He'd be there when she woke up, when she went to sleep, in her face. All day. "It's not feasible. You have a company to run. You can't trail after me on an hour-to-hour basis."

Her suitcase hit the floor with a heavy thud. Reame folded his arms across that continent-size chest and tilted his head. "You're nervous."

Well, duh.

"You don't need to be," Reame told her, using a voice that could sooth wild horses. "Despite what happened earlier, nothing is going to happen between us. You're now my client and that means that you are untouchable.

"If my employees crossed a line like that with their principals they'd get fired. I hold myself to the same standards I do them," Reame said, avoiding her eyes. His words were meant to reassure her, so why was she feeling thwarted? Really, none of this made any sense. "Besides, if it makes you feel any better, you're not my type."

God help the women he kissed who were his type. "I'm not?"

"Firstly, you're Linc's sister and I don't fool around with my good friends' sisters because brothers tend to get pissed off. Secondly, I don't do commitment and I only fool around with women who fool around too, who have no expectations beyond a fun time." Linc ran his hand over his face. "That kiss earlier was a…"

"Mistake." Lachlyn filled in the word for him, feeling like she'd run a marathon or swum the English Channel.

"Yeah, it was a mistake," Reame agreed. "It won't happen again."

Lachlyn knew that she shouldn't be feeling the level of disappointment she did and couldn't understand why. This was the smart option, the sensible choice. This was what she wanted!

"Now that we've got that settled, can we go?" Reame demanded, picking up her suitcase again. He glanced down at it, frowned and pushed it away. "I'll come back for that later tonight, when the crowd goes to bed. If they see you leaving with a suitcase, they'll follow and that's exactly what you don't want. Anything in there you can't live without?"

Yes, her lingerie and her toiletry bag and her pile of books. Lachlyn gasped when Reame tossed the case onto its back, crouched down and flipped the lid open. Her lingerie, her one indulgence apart from books, was the last thing she'd packed. Lachlyn blushed as Reame looked down at her pink camouflage bra, bright purple thong and almost transparent lacy boy-cut panties.

She saw him swallow once, then twice, before standing up and gesturing to the frothy, jewel-colored piles. "Grab whatever you need and shove it into your bag. One of my guys will bring the rest over later tonight."

Lachlyn nodded, crouched down and balanced on her toes. She grabbed two matching sets of lingerie, a T-shirt, her toiletry bag and three books. She just managed to squeeze them all into her leather tote bag. She shut the suitcase, closed the hinges and stood up.

Reame held out his hand to take her tote bag.

"I can carry it," Lachlyn assured him.

Reame nodded. "After I open the door, stay behind me, keep hold on my hand. Do not speak, not even to say no comment."

Lachlyn nodded. "I know the drill. Shoot, my sunglasses!"

She needed her glasses because the winter sun was bright but mostly because she knew that she still looked like a haunted rabbit whenever she faced the press. Pulling open the side of her bag, she dug in and rootled around, unable to lay her hands on her shades. Dammit. Grabbing a handful of lingerie, she handed it to Reame to hold, then passed him two books, another bra, a T-shirt and her toiletry bag. And another book. She peered into the depths, shook her bag and saw her glasses under her purse. She pulled them out, jammed them onto the top of her head and looked at Reame, who was holding the bundle of silk and satins, paperbacks and a hard copy, her toiletry bag dangling off his index finger. Seeing his big hands holding her intimate clothing sent a bolt of warmth through her, straight to her core. Dammit, she had to stop allowing him to do that to her.

She wasn't his type and he was more than she wanted to deal with. Too big, too intense, too alive.

Too tempting, too uncontrollable, too fascinating.

Far too dangerous...

*Just cool yourself and use your brain, Latimore.*

Lachlyn opened her bag wide and gestured for Reame to dump her stuff back into its depths. He did and Lachlyn managed to smile, enjoying seeing him looking uncomfortable for once. "Shall we go?" she asked.

Reame scrubbed his hands over his face before reaching for the door handle. "Yeah. Remember, look straight ahead and don't speak."

"And keep hold of your hand."

Reame's eyes blazed as her hand slid into his,

their fingers entwined. "I'm not going to let you go, Lachlyn."

He meant for the short walk to the car he had waiting, Lachlyn thought as he opened the front door and the crowd roared their questions. Not for anything more than that. Because, thanks to her past, that was impossible.

# Five

Reame found a parking for his black SUV a block from Lachlyn's apartment. He exited his vehicle to walk around the hood to open her door for her. Lachlyn hopped down, pulling her oversize tote bag—full of the bits and pieces of silk and satin he'd been trying, very hard, not to think about—over her shoulder.

But images of the very blonde Lachlyn wearing nothing more than a vibrant-colored bra and matching panties that wouldn't fit a flea kept jumping into his head. He wanted to pull aside silky material to see her creamy nipple and push scraps of lace—designed to be panties but could be used as a weapon of distraction—down her legs.

Lachlyn slammed the passenger door and the sound pulled Reame back to the present. Great bodyguard he was... He was supposed to be watching Lachlyn's back but he was far more interested in fantasizing about what was under her clothes. The

US government had spent millions training him to be aware of his surroundings to prepare for anything and everything, to anticipate situations before they arose. And here he was in fantasy land.

This had to stop…

Reame scanned the area but didn't see anything or anyone that lifted the hairs on the back of his neck. Best of all, he saw no press, which meant that his computer guy had covered Lachlyn's cyber tracks well and no one had her address yet.

Lachlyn pulled her bag over her shoulder and turned right, heading down the block. Coffee shop, tailor and dry cleaning, second-hand book shop. Deli, a Filipino restaurant. So far, so good. "How long have you lived in this area?" Reame asked her, pulling her out of the way of an incoming skateboarder.

Lachlyn pushed her heavy bangs out of her eyes and tucked the hair behind her ear. He'd loved her long, waist-length hair but this short, sassy style was growing on him. "About four years." She looked around and a small smile touched her amazing lips.

"It's cheap, diverse and safe. I can get to Midtown in thirty minutes." Lachlyn gestured to an Irish pub across the road. "Best burgers in the city."

Reame lifted his eyebrows at the challenge. "I know where all the good burgers in the city are."

Lachlyn lifted her thumb at a nondescript restaurant to her right. "Best Thai food in the city."

"You're making a lot of claims, Latimore."

"I can back them up," Lachlyn responded. "I'm

a lousy cook so I eat out a lot. I'm an adventurous eater so this area suits me well."

He couldn't help wondering whether she was equally adventurous in bed. Yeah, he shouldn't be thinking about her like that but he was a red-blooded, horny man and she was five feet of undiluted sexiness.

*You really need to get laid, Jepsen.* One night, a few nights, weeks, pure sex, just pleasure with no responsibilities. He seriously needed to put himself out of his misery and go on a frickin' date!

Reame followed Lachlyn into an Italian bakery and the smell of butter and sugar hit his nose. His stomach rumbled, and he suddenly remembered that he hadn't had anything to eat all day except for a green smoothie after his gym session much earlier in the day.

*"Ciao, bella."* Reame heard the boisterous greeting and saw Lachlyn lifting a hand to return it but he veered away and headed for the display fridges, his mouth watering. Cannelloni, ricotta cheesecake, pasticiotti. There was also herb and garlic focaccia and he could easily imagine tearing the bread apart, steam rising, and eating it straight from the oven. Before his parents moved, they'd lived in Flushing, another diverse neighborhood with many mom-and-pop food businesses, and like Lachlyn, he was an adventurous eater.

He was also an adventurous lover and, judging by the way she kissed, he thought she might be, as well. Not that he'd ever get to put that theory to the test…

"Reame?"

Reame wrenched his eyes away from the bomboloni—Italian doughnuts—and saw that Lachlyn was behind the counter, waiting for him to follow her. He hurried across the room, pausing when Lachlyn introduced him to Riccardo, a tall, thin man who Lachlyn said was both the baker and owner. Reame followed Lachlyn into the heart of the bakery and up a narrow flight of stairs.

"Two flights up," Lachlyn said, jogging up the stairs.

"You access your apartment through the bakery?" Reame asked.

"Ric lives on the first-floor apartment, I'm on the top floor. There is another entrance at the back of the building but this is easier, and doesn't require me to walk around the building and down a dark alley."

"Good plan," Reame said as they hit the second set of stairs. "Did you ask Riccardo whether anyone had been by looking for you during the past week?"

"I spoke to him shortly before we left The Den and he said no," Lachlyn replied and Reame had a hard time keeping his eyes off her exceptional butt and long, shapely legs.

Strange that nobody in the bakery had contacted the press to tell them where she lived, that they knew her. Despite his guy covering her tracks, he would've expected some press to have picked up her trail. Weird, Reame thought, as, out of the corner of his eye, he caught sight of a shadow passing over the wall at the top of the stairs. Reame reacted instinctively, clamping his hand around Lachlyn's wrist and jerking her down the steps. She yelped as he pushed her behind him, creating a barrier between him and the three camera-wielding journalists at the top of the stairs.

"How much money are the Ballantynes giving you?"

"Are you moving back in?"

"How does it feel to be one of the wealthiest women in the city?"

Reame cursed, spun around and pushed Lachlyn down the stairs and they burst into the bakery, straight into a bigger crowd. Ric had set this up, Reame realized. They'd been waiting…somewhere. Reame wrapped his arm around Lachlyn and marched them toward the front door, using his height and strength to bulldoze his way through the crowd.

"I need clothes, Reame," Lachlyn said, her words barely discernible over the loud questions being fired at them from every direction.

Reame bent down to speak in her ear, tightening the grip on her arm. "I'll send someone to pack for you. Right now, I need to get you out of here."

"Who did this?" Lachlyn asked him, her eyes wide with fear and frustration.

"Who do you think, Lach? Who is the only person who would've allowed this to happen?" Reame replied.

Lachlyn spun out of his grip and he knew that she was looking for Riccardo, who was standing behind the counter. He followed her gaze and saw the smirk on his face. It was as he thought—ratting Lachlyn out was fantastic publicity. He'd have the bakery's name in every column in every paper in the morning. When Riccardo just lifted his shoulders in an "I gotta do what I gotta do" shrug, hurt swept over Lachlyn's face. *Bastard*. Reame cursed silently and slapped his hand on the door, very close to the ear of a reporter who was trying to stop them from leaving.

Reame looked down, adrenaline coursing and anger for Lachlyn heating his blood. "Swear to God, you either move or I'm putting you through the glass."

Something in his face or tone must've told the paparazzi that he was looking for an excuse to punch someone because the reporter ducked under his arm and scuttled out of the way.

Reame tugged Lachlyn through the door and hurried her down the street, the paparazzi a bunch of vultures following them all the way to his vehicle.

"Ric set me up," Lachlyn said in a small voice as they made their way back to Manhattan.

"Yep."

"I thought he was my friend," Lachlyn said, her words icy with hurt and disappointment. "Why would he do that?"

Lachlyn caught Reame's astonished look. "They offered him money or publicity, Lachlyn. The three guys at the top of the hall offered him the most."

"So he sold me out for a couple of hundred bucks?" Lachlyn asked, sounding bitter.

"Or thousands," Reame replied.

Lachlyn placed her fist in the space between her ribs, her heart still threatening to beat out of her chest. She and Ric had shared coffee and pastries, dinners, books. If one of his staff had sold her out, she could understand it, but the guilty look on his face as they left his bakery told her everything she needed to know. Her friend, one of the very few she'd allowed herself to have, had tipped off the press at her expense. It was just another reminder of why engaging with people, trusting anyone, even on a superficial basis, was a really stupid idea.

Lachlyn rested her head on the window and closed her eyes. She was so tired, emotionally and physically whipped.

Reame placed his hand on her thigh and squeezed. "Well, you need to put it behind you because we have a decision to make."

Lachlyn groaned loudly, secretly hoping that Reame wouldn't remove his hand, not just yet. It felt rather…wonderful. Despite the denim separating them, she felt heat slide into her veins. Her eyes flew open to find Reame looking at her with all the passion and need he felt for her. Lachlyn dimly realized that they had stopped for a red light and suspected that she was a heartbeat away from being hauled onto his lap and kissed senseless.

Lachlyn stayed where she was, the tips of her fingers lightly resting on the top of Reame's hand.

"God, one look at you and I forget that you are under siege from the press, that you are under my protection, that you are Linc's sister," Reame stated, his words rough and hard. "I forget that I don't mess around with my clients."

"I'm not your client—" Lachlyn began to protest but knew that she was on shaky ground indeed. Reame had been a solid barrier between her and the press. If he hadn't been there earlier she might've found herself in a situation she couldn't handle.

Their heat and chemistry was another situation she was struggling to deal with.

"Define 'mess around,'" Lachlyn whispered.

"That covers anything from kissing to raucous sex," Reame retorted, pulling his hand out from under hers to push his hair off his face.

"Okay."

"I'm serious, Lachlyn. Yeah, hooking up with you would be that easy but you are not only my client, you are my best friend's baby sister," Reame stated, his tone suggesting that she not argue.

Lachlyn knew that he wouldn't be dissuaded. And why was she so concerned what Reame Jepsen thought anyway? She wasn't going to sleep with him. She didn't sleep with random hot guys. Or any guys…

Ignoring her promise to keep herself emotionally isolated—if she didn't engage, she couldn't be hurt or disappointed—Reame was, as he kept reminding her, Linc's oldest friend. He was going to be in Linc's life for the rest of his life and that would mean seeing him occasionally, having to interact with him at the family functions she was invited to. If they did sleep together, those future occasions would be ridiculously awkward.

Awkward? They would be hell!

What was wrong with her? This wasn't like her, going into free fall because of a man. She'd, hopefully temporarily, lost her job and her way of life. She had so much to adjust to. Why was she tying herself up in knots over a man?

This was her life… She was always and forever in control of what did and did not happen in it.

"Where are we going?" Lachlyn asked suddenly, taking notice of their surroundings. They had crossed the Brooklyn Bridge and instead of heading toward the Upper West Side, Reame pointed the car toward Midtown. She sat up straight and frowned. "Why aren't you taking me to The Den?"

"That's where the press would expect you to go and they will be waiting for you there."

"So are you taking me to a hotel?"

Reame shook his head, whipped onto a side street and then into an underground parking garage. He lowered his visor, hit a button and the heavy boom in front of the car lifted.

"Where are we?"

"My place."

Lachlyn saw parking spots designated Jepsen & Associates and Reame parked in the empty space close to the elevator. The other parking space held a matte-black superbike and on the other side of that, a low-slung, German-engineered sports car. Nice.

Lachlyn released her seat belt, the back passenger

door opened and Reame grabbed her tote bag before opening her door. Lachlyn hopped down to the floor and after locking the car, Reame steered her to an elevator also marked Jepsen & Associates. He plugged a code into the keypad and the doors silently opened.

Lachlyn felt panic coat her throat. This was entirely out of her comfort zone.

"Reame, I'm really tired. I'd like to find a hotel and collapse so if we could make this trip to your office quick, I'd appreciate it," Lachlyn said, slumping against the back panel of the elevator.

"No hotel, Lachlyn. You're staying here tonight. And for the foreseeable future," Reame replied, hitting a button with the side of his fist. He tossed her a small smile. "Don't worry, I'm not going to ask you to sleep on a desk. My apartment is on the penthouse floor."

Lachlyn felt her throat close while her lungs tried to crawl out of her chest. "Uh—"

"Relax, Lach, despite the craziness between us, I'm not moving you into my bed. My apartment is on the top floor and next to it I have a fully outfitted guest suite for unexpected visitors or high-value clients who need special protection. You're going to move in there for a while until this madness dies down.

"My building is super-secure, there is no chance of anyone finding you here or sneaking in without a half dozen ex-soldiers knowing about it. If you want to go out, either I or Liam, my right-hand guy, can escort you where you need to go, depending on our schedule."

Reame sounded like he was trying to convince himself as much as he was trying to convince her. While she felt calmer hearing that she wasn't going to be staying with Reame, she would feel a lot more comfortable with more space between them. Physically and emotionally. A thousand miles might work. "I think that a hotel would be better, Reame."

Reame looked at her with hooded eyes. "Better for our attraction problem, sure. But safer? No way in hell is a hotel a safer place for you to be. Your safety will always be my paramount concern."

Lachlyn forced the words out. "Then what are we going to do about our attraction problem?"

"Hell if I know. All I know is that you are driving me crazy."

Reame leaned sideways, bent his head and Lachlyn held her breath thinking that he was about to kiss her. She titled her head and licked her bottom lip, not able to resist him. Man, she was in a heap of trouble. Reame just brushed his lips against the shell of her ear and his words vibrated off her skin.

"You are so damn beautiful," Reame told her, his voice igniting sparks on her skin.

"You smell so damn good," Lachlyn told him, standing on her toes to nuzzle her nose against his jaw. "And so are you…beautiful, I mean."

Reame's mouth curved against her ear and she felt him smiling. That smile traveled down her throat, onto her nipples and wandered down…and then down some more. She wanted to feel that smile on her lips, his tongue tangling with hers. Lachlyn turned her lips and connected with his and she felt his surprise and his hesitation. Not wanting to give him time to think, her tongue swiped his lower lip before she tugged that sexy piece of him between her teeth and nibbled. His hands found her jaw and Lachlyn swallowed his groan, entranced by the fact that this man—sexy, successful, so damn hot—wanted her.

Reame took control of their kiss, his hand moving from her jaw to the back of her head to hold her in place. He tipped her head to one side to change the angle and intensity of the kiss and she could taste his frustration, his need, his banked desire.

Reame tasted hers, feasted on her for a long minute before he pulled back and rested his forehead on hers, his light eyes frustrated but determined.

"We are not going to do this. I am not looking for this."

"Looking for what?" Lachlyn asked, her brain cells trying to restart.

"Sweet, hot…you." Reame pulled away from her, his hands holding the handrail in a death grip.

"I want hot, hard, sweaty, no-expectation sex from someone who wants to give it to me. Someone who knows the score, who can walk away with no regrets." Reame sucked in an agitated breath and his tense shoulders rose and fell.

His words were like rubber bullets peppering her skin. "And you think I want more from you?"

"It doesn't matter what you think you want, Lachlyn," Reame said, his voice harsh. "I've waited for this time, Lachlyn. I damn well deserve it. I've spent the last ten years paying bills, working my ass off, trying to be the good older brother, the responsible son, putting everyone else's needs first. This is my time, Lachlyn."

Reame turned to look at her again, his eyes blazing. "You, me…we're business, Lachlyn. You remember that, okay?"

Lachlyn placed her fist into her sternum in an attempt to push away the pool of acid there. Shooting steel into her spine, she lifted her chin and narrowed her eyes. "Since you are the one who keeps touching me, why don't you take your own advice, Jepsen?"

# Six

Two days later, on Sunday morning, Lachlyn awoke to a text from Reame inviting her to join him for breakfast. Although she loved her own company and Reame's apartment was set up to keep his guests entertained, she was desperate to leave the building, for a change of scenery and some fresh air. She'd even put up with Jepsen's company if it meant taking a break from the white walls and white furniture. Lachlyn tugged on a pair of dark jeans, tucked them into knee-high boots and pulled on a thigh-length cable-knit sweater, the blue of the sweater repeated in a blue-and-white-checked cotton scarf. Lachlyn worked her long bangs into two braids and pinned them back under her hair, totally changing her pixie cut from sophisticated to relaxed. Mascara, a hint of bronzer and lip gloss... She didn't want Reame to think that she was trying to impress him...

*You're not being businesslike*, Lachlyn chided

herself. The problem was that businesslike was the last word she'd use to describe how she felt about Reame Jepsen.

"Cut it out," Lachlyn grumbled as she walked the few steps to Reame's door. Yes, he kissed like a dream. Yes, she loved his hands on her skin but, even if he wanted to, she couldn't go there. Reame was so big, so capable…such a "take charge and get it done" type of guy. He was the pillar that supported Linc and, she imagined, the rest of the Ballantyne crew. He was the tall tree in a howling wind, the place where his friends and family could always find shelter. Calm, proficient, steadfast. She might want to sleep with him, and she reluctantly—and regretfully—admitted that she needed his bodyguarding skills, but nothing else. She was an independent, strong, capable woman who didn't need emotional and mental support. She'd be her own tree, build her own shelter.

She just needed him to take her out of the building, he didn't even have to talk to her. In fact, it would be better if he didn't…

Lachlyn knocked on the door, heard Reame's shout to come in and stepped into his private space. His apartment was a lot bigger than she thought, she realized, as she walked into the foyer. Through the open door on her right she saw a laundry room and to her left was a short passageway that ended in what looked like a bedroom the size of her apartment in Woodside. Lachlyn walked into the open-plan area, which culminated in a chef's kitchen and a combined dining and living space. His oversize man couches in deep, rich jewel colors faced tall windows. Lachlyn took another look and realized that the doors could fold back and that the living area would then flow onto the good-size balcony beyond. Lachlyn walked past Reame's furniture, noticed one of her brother's paintings on the wall and his sculpture in the corner—the man had taste and money—and placed her hand on the glass door. Sunbeams from a weak March sun tried to break through the clouds. Gray day or not, his view was spectacular. Hearing footsteps, Lachlyn turned around and saw Reame walking out from a room on the other side of the foyer and, judging from the desk she caught a glimpse of, presumed it was his home office.

"Hi," Reame said, his eyes scanning her. Dressed in an untucked green-and-white-checked shirt and well-fitting jeans, he looked spectacular. All golden goodness...

*Business*, Lachlyn reminded herself.

"How are you? Anything you need?" Reame asked her, moving to the kitchen, his bare feet silent on the hardwood flooring.

"I'm fine, thank you."

"Coffee?"

Reame pushed a mug under the spout of his coffee machine and hit a button. Lachlyn heard the grinding of beans and the smell of coffee intermingled pleasantly with his clean apartment and Reame's just-showered scent.

"How are you finding the guest suite?"

"Fine." It was a perfectly adequate word so she'd used it again.

Reame smiled. "Liar. The guest suite is very white and very cold. It was purposefully designed like that."

Lachlyn walked over to the freestanding kitchen counter and leaned her forearms on the mottled granite. "It was? Why?"

"We occasionally use it for very high-value clients who either want to drop completely off the grid for a couple of days or clients who need to drop out of sight. But it's not a place I want people to linger in so I made it as cold and as uninviting as possible."

While Lachlyn appreciated the loan of his apartment, she knew that she couldn't spend a lot of time in it. And time was the one thing she had on her hands at the moment. If she stayed in his guest apartment, she didn't need a bodyguard—or to pay Reame for one—on a minute-by-minute basis but it did mean living in what felt like a psych ward or hospital room.

Lachlyn thanked him for the cup of coffee he placed by her hands. Beggars can't be choosers, she reminded herself. At least she wasn't sharing the space with anyone; that would be a nightmare.

"You're frowning," Reame said. "What's the problem?"

"Tomorrow is Monday and I wish I had a job to go to in the morning but my supervisor nixed that idea," Lachlyn said, still upset by that decision. Somebody else would be allocated her Parisian art critic project and would make the decisions on what had historical value.

"Tell me about your work."

Normally a command like that immediately dried up her words but they were still there, bubbling on her tongue. She couldn't understand it—why him and why now?

Lachlyn shrugged. "I'm just annoyed that I can't work. I've just started sorting through a collection of diaries and documents from the Années folles— that's the crazy years of the 1920s in Paris. The collection has just arrived and I was super-excited to work on it." Lachlyn rested her forearms on the kitchen counter, thinking about the treasures she'd had to leave behind.

"What's so special about it?" Reame asked, sounding genuinely interested.

This wasn't anything personal so Lachlyn gave herself permission to ramble on. "Maxwell Cummings-Brown was an American living in Paris. Lots of money, lots of pizzazz. He was on first-name terms with Max Ernst and Salvador Dali, and it was said that he watched Josephine Baker dance the Charleston—practically naked—at the Folie Bergère. He bought jewelry from Cartier and Frédéric Boucheron for both his male and female lovers. Best of all, he kept everything—menus, calling cards, letters, diaries… It's like a snapshot of that era."

"I actually have no idea what an archivist actually does. So you get this collection in a couple of boxes—"

"Sometimes by the truckload," Lachlyn corrected him.

"And then?" Reame asked.

"Basically, I organize and rehouse the collection, whipping it into shape. Then I describe the collection so that researchers can access information easily. I specialize in late nineteenth and early twentieth century history so the Parisian collection is, was, right up my alley." Lachlyn blew out a long breath. "So instead of doing my job, I'm wafting in the breeze or, more accurately, staring at your white walls."

Reame cocked his head and Lachlyn could see the wheels turning in his head. "What if I found you another collection to whip into shape?"

Lachlyn sent him a "you're dreaming" look. She didn't want to offend him but she doubted that Reame could conceptualize the range and depth of what she normally dealt with. She didn't sort through boxes of photographs and make timelines. "I appreciate the thought," she said, choosing her words carefully, "but you can't just rustle up a collection."

Reame sent her a smile that reached her toes. "Wanna bet?"

Later that morning Lachlyn found herself walking past the exquisitely decorated windows of Ballantyne's on Fifth, her head covered in a burgundy floppy hat, oversize sunglasses on her face. Reame, dressed in faded jeans and a battered leather jacket, kept his hand on her lower back, his eyes constantly scanning the sidewalk.

Lachlyn wanted a closer look at a magnificent pearl and diamond choker in the display window but Reame wouldn't let her stop. "What's the hurry?" she demanded. "It's Sunday, the day of rest."

"Although it's early, this is also the busiest street in Manhattan and the chances of you being recognized are stratospheric. I'd like to get you off the street."

"I'd like breakfast," Lachlyn grumbled. After their discussion about her job back at his apartment, Reame had left the kitchen, headed into his den and closed the door. Taking that as a sign that he didn't want to be disturbed, and that breakfast wasn't high on his list of priorities, Lachlyn had taken her coffee onto his amazing balcony and watched Midtown rumble to life. Fifteen minutes later, Reame had emerged and told her that they were going out.

And he still hadn't fed her.

Lachlyn tried to ignore her growling stomach as Reame took her hand and stepped up to the doorway of Ballantyne's on Fifth. The door clicked open and Reame stood back to let her walk through the door first.

Because the store was opening to the public in fifteen minutes, the iconic shop was empty, blissfully quiet, with just one staff member behind the far counter. Gemstones and jewelry glittered and sparkled from their beds in the art deco display cabinets. The lighting was subtle, expensive but most of all flattering, to the customers and to the product. Tasteful and expensive artworks lined the wall and there were vases of lilies on pedestals in each corner. Lachlyn inhaled deeply and held her breath, lifting her eyebrows when she caught Reame looking at her.

"What are you doing?"

Lachlyn released her breath and lifted one shoulder. "I just love the smell of fresh flowers." She looked around and lifted her hands. "What are we doing here?"

"You'll see," Reame replied, doing his Mr. Mysterious thing. He reached for her hand and tugged her across the store, heading for a door discreetly marked Staff Only.

"Please tell me that whatever you are up to involves food," Lachlyn begged.

He grinned. "Stop whining, woman." Reame punched in the code on the access panel and then pushed open the heavy reinforced door.

"You have the access code to Ballantyne's?"

"It's a temporary code, valid for eight hours," Reame explained as they headed toward two elevators at the end of the hallway. But she still didn't understand why she was here and, more important, why he wasn't feeding her instead of taking her on a tour of the back rooms of Ballantyne International.

Before she could make another demand for an explanation, Reame stopped in front of the smaller of the two elevators. The bigger elevator was standard, with up and down arrows, but its smaller sibling had another of those damn keypads Reame was so fond of. Reame put in a code, the doors opened and they stepped inside the small box. It was way too small for two people, Lachlyn thought, her shoulder pressing into Reame's bicep. Reame placed his hand on her hip and shifted so that her back was to his front. The doors whispered closed and Reame reached past her to hit the last button in a row.

Conscious of his hand on her hip, his hard body behind her, Lachlyn tried to regulate her breathing. She could smell his sweet breath, could feel his hard chest against her back. If she pushed her bottom back she could rub against his...

Lachlyn released a huge sigh and at the same time her stomach growled, filling the small space with its demands for food.

Reame's low laugh brushed her hair. "Hungry?"

"That's what I've been telling you!" Lachlyn spun around to glare at him. Not having anywhere else to put her hands, she slapped them on his chest. "You promised me breakfast!"

Reame lifted his hand and with one finger, pushed a bang off her face. "This is better, I promise."

His eyes dipped to her mouth and he bent his finger to rub his knuckle over the ridge of her cheekbone. "You have the most beautiful skin," Reame murmured, his voice husky. "It's pure cream."

Lachlyn pushed her face into his hand, just like a cat begging to be scratched. Reame moved his thumb across her lower lip. He pressed his thumb into the center of her lip and released a heartfelt groan. Reame rested his forehead on hers.

"You're a client, Lachlyn."

"Not really," Lachlyn whispered as the elevator

stopped. She felt a cool blast of air on her back, indicating that the doors were open.

"Yeah, you are. And if you weren't, you're still my best friend's little sister."

"Not that, either," Lachlyn said. Well, she wasn't, not in the truest sense of the word. She was someone they'd just met. A sister implied that you had a history together, shared memories of a childhood spent together. She and the Ballantyne siblings would never be closer than what they currently were. She'd never allow it. She wasn't that brave. Or stupid.

"Thirdly, I only want to fool around and you're not the fool-around type," Reame said, keeping his voice low.

Lachlyn narrowed her eyes, annoyed. "That's a pretty big assumption, Jepsen. Maybe a red-hot, brief affair is exactly what I want, the only thing I need."

Such a lie but worth it if it wiped that smirk off his face...

Reame stepped back and had the audacity to deepen his smile. "So you are telling me that we could have wild sex in the limo on the way to dinner with your siblings and when we arrived at The Den, you could act like nothing happened? Cool, composed, not giving the smallest hint that I'd just had you screaming my name ten minutes before?"

Well, when he put it like that... Lachlyn scowled. "No, I couldn't pull that off." Partially because she'd never had a proper orgasm before. She released a heavy sigh, knowing that she wasn't fooling him.

"I'm not that sophisticated. Is that your definition of wild sex? Limo sex?"

"I have others."

Lachlyn blushed at the undisguised passion in his eyes.

"I'm attracted to you, Lachlyn. I'm not going to deny that, but you're not what I'm looking for."

"And that is?"

"Uncomplicated, easy, someone who just wants to have a good time. I want to be able to jump onto a dating app, to call someone at ten at night, someone who would be keen to have a drink, hit a club and then her bedroom. I want to be able to leave when we're done, guilt-free, and not have to stress about calling her the next morning. Or ever again," Reame said, putting more distance between them. "Right now I need a woman I don't have to worry about, whose feelings aren't going to be hurt if I don't call or text. I want the freedom to not have to worry about her. I'm taking a break from responsibility."

His mouth was spouting one thing but behind his bravado, she sensed a sliver of fear. This man had his own demons. "That's not you," Lachlyn said, her words falling into the silence between them.

"What do you mean?" Reame barked, nudging her out of the elevator.

Lachlyn stepped into a well-lit, stark hallway and looked around. On her right, cardboard boxes abutted a heavy, partially open steel door.

"Where are we?" Lachlyn asked, her nose immediately picking up the odors of paper and age, dust and damp.

"In the basement," Reame retorted. Lachlyn started to move toward the door but Reame caught her elbow and halted her progress. "What did you mean, Lachlyn?"

Oh God, she didn't want to talk about this anymore. She wasn't a fan of people psychoanalyzing her so she tried not to do it to other people. Reame was calm and controlled, strong-willed and dutiful. He seemed to like organization and structure. He wasn't impulsive or impetuous and she really couldn't see him in a club environment, buying drinks and spinning lines.

"That club-hopping, free-wheelin' guy isn't who you are. Neither is the have-sex-in-the-limo guy. It's too chaotic."

"You don't know me."

"Fair point," Lachlyn conceded. "But I find it interesting that you use the words *I* and *want* a lot… 'I want to do this, I want to do that.' You're good-looking, rich, successful. So why aren't you doing it?"

Lachlyn pushed her hand through her hair, and the corners of her mouth lifted. "I respect the fact that I'm not your type and I'm okay with it. God knows that my life is complicated enough at the moment. Can I just ask one last thing?"

Reame's expression hardened and she saw impatience flash in his eyes. He was fully uncomfortable with this topic but he was too polite to ask her to shut the hell up.

"Is there food behind door number one?"

\* \* \*

The last and only time he'd visited this basement storage area was when he was first employed by Connor, a few weeks after he was discharged from the army. Connor had a rather fluid idea of what a bodyguard should do and wasn't afraid to add extraneous duties to his job description. He'd picked up dry cleaning, occasionally acted as chauffeur to Connor's lady friends, done some heavy lifting. He hadn't minded. Connor had paid him a hefty salary that'd allowed him to clear the most pressing debts his dad had left behind and allowed him to catch up on his mom's mortgage payments for her house.

He'd accompanied Connor to this room and his boss had told him to find a book of hand-drawn jewelry designs from the '50s. Hetty Clark-Grimbly wanted him to re-create the engagement ring he designed for her mother, which she'd lost while swimming off a private yacht in the Med. *Find the book, dear boy*, he'd said.

The dear boy had searched for two days solid through generations of Ballantyne crap before Connor blithely told him that he'd found the book in the study at The Den, the day before.

Reame was fond of Connor but he'd come close to throttling him that day. The massive room was even fuller today than back then, boxes and odd bits of furniture scattered across the cold concrete floor. One corner of the room held props and old window decorations, there were paintings leaning against the walls. But mostly there were boxes and more boxes.

Messy, disorganized, dusty…it offended Reame's organized military soul. But Lachlyn looked like she had stepped into the lost Library of Alexandria.

"Lachlyn Latimore, meet the Ballantynes' junk room," Reame said, leaning his shoulder into the door frame. "Your new project."

Lachlyn blinked at him, her eyes foggy. "What?"

"The idea popped into my head when we were talking about your work at the NYPL," Reame explained. "As you might have realized, I spend a lot of time with the Ballantyne siblings. Over the years, there has been a raging argument about what to do with this room, specifically the stuff in this room. They keep promising to get it done, that they have to sort this mess out, that the Ballantyne history—most of which is in here—has to be preserved. Every couple of years, they traipse down here, determined to sort it out."

"Then they take one look at it and find something more important to do?"

Reame nodded. "Exactly." Reame walked farther into the room and scowled. "God, it's a mess. I don't remember it being this bad but when I spoke to Beck earlier, he said that early last year, a container of boxes came from the Ballantyne jewelry store in London, as they were running out of space. The store above us opened in the 1890s. London opened a few months later. So some of this stuff is old."

"What sort of materials are we talking about, Reame? Letters? Accounts? Diaries?"

"I asked Beck that and he said anything and everything. Signage, designs, smalls. Personal and professional stuff from the Ballantynes' past." Reame shoved his hands into the back pockets of his jeans. "You need something to keep you occupied in the day, Lach, and that would help me. This building is like Fort Knox. There's no safer place for you to be. I can drop you off in the morning, pick you up in the evening and you can putter around in here to your heart's content." Reame kept his voice low, reminding himself not to push. "You'd also get a really good idea of the family you are now part of."

Lachlyn rocked on her heels. "And the siblings are happy about me doing this?"

Reame laughed. "Happy? Well, handing over first-born children and sacrifices to the gods were mentioned if you took on this task." Reame rubbed the back of his neck, wondering how to frame his next comment. He wasn't a subtle guy so he'd just come out and say it. "They said that they'd pay you to do it."

Lachlyn's back stiffened and those bright blue eyes turned frosty. "In addition to the forty million?"

That much? Holy hell. Reame didn't react. "Can I point out that all the Ballantynes work for the company and they all get paid a monthly salary to do that? Linc offering you money to do a job, a job you have the skills for, is not an insult."

Lachlyn lowered her eyes and he saw the pink tinge of embarrassment on her face. He'd been totally wrong when he assumed that she was just out for the Ballantyne cash; that had been a major misjudgment on his part. Lachlyn was turning out to be deeper and more complicated than he'd expected.

And far more perceptive than he'd expected. Her earlier question about why he kept talking about having this hot affair, this responsibility-free lifestyle and not doing what he said rocked him. He wasn't the type of guy who said one thing and did another so why hadn't he gone on a date yet? What was holding him back? He had the time and the opportunity…he just needed to get his ass into gear.

Make a connection, take a girl out for a drink, to dinner. Get laid. *This isn't nuclear fusion, Jepsen.*

And none of those plans had to, or would, include Lachlyn. He turned to look at her and smiled when he saw her sitting on the dusty floor, quickly sorting through a pile of papers, abruptly pushing her bangs behind her ears when they obscured what she was reading.

Reame pulled out his vibrating cell phone and looked down at the flashing screen. He opened the Ballantyne family chat group and skimmed through the multiple messages.

Did Lachlyn take the bait? Is she going to do it? Please tell me she said yes.

Reame looked at Lachlyn again and his heart skipped a beat when he caught her tracing a finger over a ragged-edged photograph. "Lach?" he quietly called.

She didn't respond so he tried again. "Lach? Breakfast time."

Lachlyn made a humming sound in response and he watched, amused, as her hand dipped into the box next to her, pulling out a wad of papers as she perused the document in her hand.

She'd forgotten about him and her growling stomach. Reame quickly typed a message on his phone.

It looks like you've got yourselves an archivist.

# Seven

Later that week, Reame knocked on the door of the guest suite, expecting it to swing open and to see Lachlyn's wide smile. When the door remained closed, he frowned and knocked again. There was nothing but silence behind the walls so he turned the knob and stepped inside. He found Lachlyn sitting on the white sofa still in her pajamas, a pile of papers on her lap.

Giving her a closer look, Reame realized that her eyes were red-rimmed. She looked exhausted. "Hey."

"Hey back." Lachlyn's smile didn't hold a fraction of its normal wattage.

He crossed the apartment and sat down on the cold, white coffee table in front of her. "Did you sleep last night?"

"Not much," Lachlyn replied.

"Are you sick?"

Lachlyn shook her head and looked down at her

flannel pajamas. "I'm sorry, I'm running late. Can you give me twenty minutes?" She sighed and started to swing her legs off the couch, her toes tipped in shell pink. Pretty toes, Reame thought. The middle one sported a toe ring. Sweet and sexy.

Reame felt the action in his pants and ignored his trigger-happy junk. He placed his hand on her slim thigh to keep her lightly pinned to the sofa. He shouldn't ask, he should keep his distance, but the words flew out of his mouth despite his best intentions. "What's the matter, Lach?"

Lachlyn picked up the sheaf of papers, straightened them by banging them to her knee and slid them back into the folder. "Linc hired me a lawyer to go through the Ballantyne offer, to answer any questions I might have that I don't feel comfortable asking them directly."

That was Linc, Reame thought, cool, capable and hell-bent on making the situation as easy as possible. "I have a meeting with her at nine thirty." Lachlyn grimaced. "Sorry, I meant to tell you but I forgot. If that doesn't suit you, I can reschedule."

The look she sent him was full of hope and Reame knew that she was trying to avoid the meeting, possibly trying to avoid the whole inheritance saga, as well. He was a confront-and-deal-with-it type of guy. He didn't avoid situations and conflicts.

Lachlyn, he suspected, did. She also avoided people. He'd heard that the Ballantyne women were desperate to take her out for a girls' night—though how much fun three pregnant women could have was debatable—but Lachlyn kept finding an excuse not to go. She was the most solitary person he'd ever met, content to spend hours on her own in the Ballantyne basement. After taking her home, she slipped into this guest apartment and, because he had to approve any visitors to this floor, he knew that no one had visited her since she moved in a week earlier. Her cell phone was monitored to keep track of the crazies and yeah, he'd peeked at her call logs. A few text messages from the Ballantyne women, Linc, two calls from Sage that didn't last more than thirty seconds each and a longer call from her brother Tyce.

The woman was a self-contained island...

If she couldn't talk to her future sister-in-law and brother, then there wasn't much chance of her opening up to a lawyer. And she needed to—this wasn't Monopoly money they were dealing with. "You need to meet with the lawyer, Lach."

Lachlyn shook her head. "Why? It seems pretty simple...they want to give me money and pass on a share of the assets."

"You make it sound like they are trying to give you a nasty infection, Lach. This isn't a bad thing."

Lachlyn jumped up and walked over to the coffeepot in the kitchen. Reame couldn't help noticing that she was braless and that her breasts were round and perfect. *Ah, crap.*

Lachlyn lifted the coffeepot in his direction. He nodded. What the hell, at least holding a cup of coffee would give him something to do with his hands.

Reame waited for Lachlyn to bring his coffee over

before gesturing for her to sit down. She did, perching on the end of the uncomfortable-looking cushion. Reame picked up his coffee mug and held it loosely between his hands. "So, why are you hesitating about taking their offer? What's stopping you?"

Reame knew that Lachlyn was thinking about changing the subject and wondered whether she'd answer. "People think it's so easy, that I should just accept their offer and slip into their family. They think that I should just jump at the chance at being part of the Ballantyne legacy."

Wow, okay, that was a genuine answer and a whole bunch of honesty he didn't expect.

"So, what's the problem, Lach?"

Lachlyn lifted her feet up to the cushion and wrapped her arms around her bent legs. "I don't know what being part of a family means, how to act, what to do." More honesty, Reame thought. This was Lachlyn raw and unedited and he felt, yeah, touched, that this intensely private woman was opening up to him.

"Tyce and I grew up hard, Reame, like really hard. It was very tough and my mom just managed to bring in just enough to cover the basics. At any given time, we were a tiny crisis away from living on the streets. My mom would come home from work and collapse in a heap, and I'm not exaggerating. She'd fall down, onto her bed or the couch and she wouldn't move, frequently she wouldn't speak, until she had to get up the next morning for work."

Reame made a sympathetic sound in the back

of his throat but kept it down. Sympathy, he knew, would not be appreciated. "Tyce got me to school and, when I was smaller, organized for me to stay with our neighbors, at the library, in shelters. Wherever he could stash me, he would—"

"There're ten years between you. Why didn't he look after you himself?" Reame asked, confused.

"Because he was constantly hustling for cash. That crack between income and expenses was sliver-thin. Tyce had to make up the shortfall. He washed windows, cars, sold his sketches…he did what he could while trying to look after me," Lachlyn explained. "Between the ages of three and maybe six or seven, I didn't know whose house I would be going to that day, whether I would know the caretaker or not. All I knew was that I had to be good, stay invisible and wait for Tyce to pick me up in the afternoon. If he was one minute late, I would start to panic."

Lachlyn looked away, staring at a point past his head. Reame rested his forearms on his thighs, not dropping his eyes from her face. If he did, he'd lose her. There was more to this story and Reame knew that if she didn't tell him now, she might never.

"My biggest dream was for a family, some normality. I held on to that dream, lived it, breathed it, was obsessed by it. Around the age of fifteen I finally accepted that it wasn't ever going to happen and I was cool with it."

Oh, now that was a lie, Reame thought. She wasn't cool with it then and she most definitely wasn't now. He really wanted to know what happened to destroy

Dear Reader,

**IT'S A FACT:** if you answer 4 quick questions, we'll send you **4 FREE REWARDS!**

I'm not kidding you. As a leading publisher of women's fiction, we value your opinions... and your time. That's why we are prepared to **reward** you handsomely for completing our mini-survey. In fact, we have 4 Free Rewards for you, including 2 free books and 2 free gifts.

As you may have guessed, that's why our mini-survey is called **"4 for 4".** Answer 4 questions and get 4 Free Rewards. It's that simple!

Thank you for participating in our survey,

*Pam Powers*

# To get your 4 FREE REWARDS:
## Complete the survey below and return the insert today to receive 2 FREE BOOKS and 2 FREE GIFTS guaranteed!

## "4 for 4" MINI-SURVEY

**1** Is reading one of your favorite hobbies?
☐ YES ☐ NO

**2** Do you prefer to read instead of watch TV?
☐ YES ☐ NO

**3** Do you read newspapers and magazines?
☐ YES ☐ NO

**4** Do you enjoy trying new book series with FREE BOOKS?
☐ YES ☐ NO

**YES!** I have completed the above Mini-Survey. Please send me my 4 FREE REWARDS (worth over $20 retail). I understand that I am under no obligation to buy anything, as explained on the back of this card.

### 225/326 HDL GMYG

FIRST NAME

LAST NAME

ADDRESS

APT.#

CITY

STATE/PROV.

ZIP/POSTAL CODE

## READER SERVICE—Here's how it works:

Accepting your 2 free Harlequin Desire® books and 2 free gifts (gifts valued at approximately $10.00 retail) places you under no obligation to buy anything. You may keep the books and gifts and return the shipping statement marked "cancel." If you do not cancel, about a month later we'll send you 6 additional books and bill you just $4.55 each in the U.S. or $5.24 each in Canada. That is a savings of at least 13% off the cover price. It's quite a bargain! Shipping and handling is just 50¢ per book in the U.S. and 75¢ per book in Canada*. You may cancel at any time, but if you choose to continue, every month we'll send you 6 more books, which you may either purchase at the discount price plus shipping and handling or return to us and cancel your subscription. *Terms and prices subject to change without notice. Prices do not include applicable taxes. Sales tax applicable in N.Y. Canadian residents will be charged applicable taxes. Offer not valid in Quebec. Books received may not be as shown. All orders subject to approval. Credit or debit balances in a customer's account(s) may be offset by any other outstanding balance owed by or to the customer. Please allow 4 to 6 weeks for delivery. Offer available while quantities last.

▲ If offer card is missing write to: Reader Service, P.O. Box 1341, Buffalo, NY 14240-8531 or visit www.ReaderService.com ▲

BUSINESS REPLY MAIL
FIRST-CLASS MAIL    PERMIT NO. 717    BUFFALO, NY

POSTAGE WILL BE PAID BY ADDRESSEE

READER SERVICE
PO BOX 1341
BUFFALO NY 14240-8571

NO POSTAGE
NECESSARY
IF MAILED
IN THE
UNITED STATES

that dream. "Twelve years later, the thing I most wanted is mine for the taking but I can't accept it. I disconnected from that dream and I can't go back there."

Her foot was a scant inch from his hand so Reame rubbed his thumb over the ball of her toe, trying to comfort her in a way that wouldn't spook her. Because this girl was already spooked to the max.

"I think that you not only disconnected from the dream, you disconnected, period. One day you might tell me what happened to cause that."

Panic flashed in her eyes and Reame cursed himself. *Too fast, too soon, idiot.* "It's easier to be alone, Reame."

"But far less fun," Reame countered.

"The Ballantynes are the most in-tune, most interconnected people I know. They communicate silently, through laughter and their eyes, their facial expressions. They all seem to operate on their own special bandwidth," Lachlyn said, waving her hands around. "You know what I mean. You do it, as well... with them.

"I can't be like that, operate like that. It's... overwhelming," Lachlyn added.

"Tyce seems to be fitting in okay," Reame stated, keeping his tone and expression calm.

Lachlyn scoffed. "He's in love with Sage. He'd do and say or be anything for her."

"Are you saying that he is faking his friendship with your brothers, with me?"

Lachlyn rubbed the back of her neck. "No, of

course I'm not! I think that this is the first time he's had friends, real friends."

"So, if he has managed to overcome his crappy childhood and find his place in the family, why can't you?" Reame asked, crossing his feet at his ankles and looking at her over the rim of his coffee cup.

"Because I'm not as strong as him, as brave." Lachlyn whipped back and Reame saw her frustration.

"It's your family, Lach. It's supposed to be the one place where you don't have to be strong or brave. It's the one place where you can let your guard down, where you don't have to be a self-contained, independent entity. Someplace where someone else can take up the slack."

Lachlyn sent him a smile so sad that it raised blisters on his heart. "I know that you probably won't understand this, but the loneliest place you can be is in a place where expectations aren't fulfilled, where the people who are supposed to love you the most can decimate you without even trying."

Reame reached out to grab her, wanting to hold her, to wipe the devastation from her face. But Lachlyn was too quick for him—she scrambled away and hurried into the hall. "I'll meet you downstairs in thirty minutes."

Staring at his empty hands, Reame cursed. He jumped up and easily caught up with her, holding her delicate wrist in his big hand. He was about to speak when her eyes connected with his and he saw her embarrassment, her fear and intense vulnerability. Bombs and bullets had never shaken him but she made him weak at the knees.

"I can't talk anymore, Reame. Please don't ask me to," Lachlyn whispered, staring down at his brown hand holding her white arm.

Reame stroked her skin with his thumb before releasing her. He wouldn't force her, he couldn't. Force was not part of his vocabulary when it came to women. So he changed the subject.

"I need this guest suite back for a couple of days. I have a high-value target who needs a place to hide out while we set up a safe house for him."

Lachlyn blinked a few times. "Safe house?"

"Yeah, he's testifying against a drug cartel and he doesn't trust the US Marshal Service to keep him safe. He's an idiot, those guys are awesome, but the guy has cash to burn and he's hired us to look after his sorry ass. So you're going to move into my guest bedroom for a few nights. Can you deal?"

He expected her to run, to insist that she go to a hotel, but after panic flashed through her eyes, he saw a touch of resignation. Maybe it was exhaustion or maybe she was finally beginning to feel more comfortable around him. Her opening up had him leaning toward the latter.

Amusement flashed in Lachlyn's eyes, surprising him. She lifted a cheeky eyebrow. "Won't I cramp your style?"

Reame narrowed his eyes at her. "I think I can cope for a few nights."

Lachlyn grinned at him and he was relieved to see

the pain in her eyes dissipating. "So have you managed to have limo sex yet?"

Well, no. Nor any other type of sex.

"You're definitely a Ballantyne," Reame muttered as he turned to walk back to the front door. It was either walk away or kiss the hell out of her. "Just another pain in my ass."

That evening, Lachlyn dumped her suitcases in Reame's guest bedroom, plugged her phone in to charge and walked into the living area of his apartment. Thirty seconds later she heard the door to Reame's bedroom open and she turned to watch him cross the floor. His hunter green T-shirt accentuated his broad shoulders, the hem of the sleeves tight around his biceps. Straight-legged track pants rode low on his hips and made his legs seem longer. He looked spectacular.

He was also, obviously, going out. So why was she feeling disappointed? Being alone was what she specialized in, wasn't it?

Lachlyn watched Reame walk into the kitchen to open the stainless steel fridge. "I've got wine and beer and water, some fruit juice."

Lachlyn heard the slow roll of her stomach and waited for him to mention food. "I really need to get some food in but help yourself to anything you find." He slammed the fridge door closed and picked up a black sweatshirt that lay on the kitchen counter, pulling it over his head.

Lachlyn perched on the arm of a leather couch,

feeling jittery and a little resentful. Who went out the first night they had a guest? Except that she wasn't a guest, she was an obligation, someone Reame was helping for Linc's sake. She was safe in his apartment, in this building. He'd fulfilled his end of the bargain.

Reame bent over to pick up a pair of trainers and Lachlyn was jolted out of her pity party when his pants pulled tight across his perfect, perfect ass. She touched her cheek with the backs of her fingers, felt the lava under her skin and frantically searched for the smallest drop of moisture in her mouth.

*Oh...oh, wow.*

Reame straightened and walked over to the opposite sofa, sitting down to pull on his shoes. He lifted his head to look at her and, damn, caught the lust on her face. His eyes narrowed, his cheeks flushed and his fingers stilled. Electricity danced over her skin, blood raced from her brain into her heart and she felt her womb contract once, then again. She wanted him, Lachlyn thought, dazed. In his hot gaze she saw his tanned hands on her light skin, could taste him on her tongue. Unconsciously, her legs spread and her core throbbed.

Reame swiped his hand over his face and released a low, dark curse. He stood up abruptly and Lachlyn saw his erection tenting his pants. He released another harsh, pithy curse before stomping toward his bedroom.

Right, so he wasn't happy about whatever was bubbling between them. She got that, she wasn't too thrilled herself. Lachlyn pushed the balls of her hands into her forehead. She was living in his space—she'd have to see a lot more of him. How were they going to keep their hands off each other? She needed to keep her distance from him—sleeping with Linc's best friend was a spectacularly bad idea.

*Oh, Bitch Fate, why him and why now? What are you trying to teach me?*

Lachlyn heard the hard knock against his door and dropped her hands. Since Reame had told her that she shouldn't, under any circumstances, open the door, she stayed where she was. "Get that, won't you?" Reame yelled from the bedroom.

Lachlyn stood up slowly and walked into the hall, checking her reflection in the mirror over the hall table. Bright eyes, flushed cheeks, wet mouth. Yeah, she looked as turned on as she felt. Irritated, she wiped her mouth with the back of her hand and ordered herself to get a grip.

*You are not going to have sex with Reame Jepsen,* she told herself. She was to live here until the press coverage died down, then she was going to exit his and the Ballantynes' lives. She turned the knob and pulled the door open. *Let's repeat this—you are definitely not going to sleep—*

"What are you mumbling about, Lach?"

Lachlyn looked up at her half brother, dressed in athletic gear. He held two boxes of pizza in one hand and Sage, as per usual, was tucked into his side.

"Uh, hi," Lachlyn said, standing back to let them in. *People*, she thought. *Damn.* "Come on in."

"Reame and I are going to work out," Tyce said, thrusting the box of pizza into Sage's hand. "Sage is hanging with you."

Lachlyn, feeling Reame's presence behind her, put her back to her brother and Sage and sent him a "save me" look. He shook his head before rolling his eyes. He placed his hands on her shoulders and dipped his head to kiss her cheek and whisper in her ear. "It's pizza. There's wine in the fridge. A little conversation with a nice person. You can do this, Latimore."

Lachlyn glared at his back as he followed Tyce into the hall. When they disappeared around the corner, she turned back to Sage, who was standing in the doorway, tears in her eyes.

"I can go, if you'd prefer," Sage stated quietly. "Reame said that there was no food in the house so I'll leave you the pizza."

Lachlyn bit her bottom lip. She hadn't meant to hurt Sage but she wasn't good at surprises. She didn't like to be ambushed. She liked to have time to prepare...

Lachlyn heard Reame's voice in her ear. *It's not war, Latimore. It's Sage, your brother's fiancée, the mother of your niece. Or nephew.*

Lachlyn shook her head and made herself reach for Sage's hand. "No, come on in. Please."

She couldn't keep ignoring the Ballantynes, they wouldn't let her, so she supposed that she was going to have to learn to deal with them. She'd have a slice of pizza, politely listen to Sage's arguments on why she should take the money, she'd agree to disagree, and then Sage would want to tell her about Connor, about the father she never knew. Lachlyn wondered where Reame kept his aspirin; she knew that she'd need a few before the night was over.

Sage's hand on her arm halted her progress back into Reame's apartment. "Lach? Can we forget, just for tonight, about the money and Connor, and me being a Ballantyne? Can I just be the girl who wants to get to know her fiancé's sister?"

Lachlyn smiled and immediately her headache receded. "That sounds so good to me."

# Eight

Reame felt the feminine hand land on his thigh and looked down at the painted pink fingernails and the expensive rings decorating that hand. It was inching higher up his leg and he waited for his junk to react, his interest to form.

Nope. Nothing.

*Crap.*

Reame turned his head to look at his date and wondered what the hell was wrong with him. He'd met Gretchen a few weeks ago on a dating app and had invited her out for a drink. Over a couple of beers, he'd found the forensic psychologist fascinating. Intelligence and sexy was a killer combination. Within an hour, they'd both known that if she hadn't been flying out that night, they would've hooked up in her hotel room for a night long on pleasure and short on regrets. She was based in Seattle but she crisscrossed the country and would like to, she'd

told him, have dinner with him the next time she
was in town.

And by dinner she meant food followed by hot,
no-strings sex.

Now here they were, in a taxi, headed toward her
hotel. The dinner had been good, her company interesting, but his body wasn't cooperating. Gretchen
was tall, buxom and confident and, he was sure,
knew her way around a man's body. She was what
he'd been wanting, looking for, but the thought of
kissing her mouth, palming her breast made him
feel a little nauseous.

Maybe he was coming down with something.

Gretchen lifted her hand off his thigh and half
turned in her seat, crossing her spectacular legs. "Are
you okay?"

Reame lifted one eyebrow at her very female
question. "I'm fine, why?"

"Well, we had a lovely meal and we enjoyed the
conversation." She tipped her head to the side, her
eyes roaming over his features. "At least, I enjoyed
myself."

"Dinner was fine, Gretchen."

"Fine. Just what every girl wants to hear,"
Gretchen replied, her tone cooling. She tapped her
clutch bag against her knee in obvious frustration. "I
thought we were on the same page, Reame."

So had he. Reame sighed, thought about fudging
his answer and decided not to, that Gretchen's confidence deserved the truth. He pushed his hair away
from his eyes and tried to smile. "I did enjoy dinner,

Gretchen. You have a fascinating job and an interesting life. You're a fascinating woman."

"A month ago, if I hadn't had a flight to catch, we
would've spent the night together."

"Yeah, we would've," Reame admitted.

"But that's not going to happen tonight, is it?"

Again, it would be so much easier to fudge. But
she deserved better. "It could," he admitted. He
shrugged and her thin eyebrows pulled together in
a frown. "I'm a guy—touch me in a couple of places
and it could happen."

"But it wouldn't be about me."

If they had sex, he'd make it good for her—of
course he would. He'd get off and she would get off
and afterward there wouldn't be anything to say because she'd know that he'd been thinking of someone
else while kissing and touching her. Women were
spooky clever that way.

"So, you're telling me that I'm not your first
choice tonight."

Reame picked up her hand and kissed her fingers.
"I'm telling you that I think that you deserve to have
someone fully there in the moment with you, enjoying you. I'm not that guy, not tonight."

Reame could see the offer of them trying this
again when she returned to the city hovering on her
lips and he hoped, prayed that she didn't utter the
words. He didn't want to tell her that he wouldn't
take her call, that their moment had passed. The
words were about to tumble out when Gretchen's
lips firmed and she nodded once, then again.

Fortuitously, her nodding coincided with the taxi pulling to a stop outside the entrance to her hotel. "I'll walk you to the door," Reame said.

He sighed when Gretchen opened her own door, ignoring the hand he held out. She seemed to realize that asking him not to walk her to the entrance was futile so he matched her long strides to where the doorman stood, the door open for them. Gretchen turned, placed her hand on his arm and her cheek against his.

"Thanks for dinner, Reame. I'm sorry this didn't work out."

"Me too." He genuinely was. Taking Gretchen to bed would've been a hundred times simpler than dealing with the blonde bundle of craziness he'd left in his apartment.

The one he actually wanted, consistently craved.

Sitting in Reame's den, Lachlyn dipped her hand into a bag of chocolate-covered peanuts and as she lifted the handful of sweets to her mouth, she heard the slam of Reame's front door, heavy footsteps crossing the floor of his apartment. Lachlyn muted the television and looked at her watch; Reame was back early from his date.

Lachlyn had thought that she'd spend a sleepless night listening for him to return, if he returned at all. So she was very surprised to hear that he was back and shortly after ten. Hearing his footsteps approaching the den, Lachlyn rolled the packet closed and shoved it down the side of the cushion. She stared at the TV, pretending total fascination. Reame's ego was healthy enough—he did not need to know that she'd spent the past three hours in agony, imagining him eating and drinking and flirting.

Lachlyn dragged her eyes off the TV as he sat down on the couch next to her, propping his flat-soled boots up onto the designer coffee table. He looked amazing in dark jeans, an expensive white shirt and soft green jacket.

"Hi. Good night?" Lachlyn asked, proud of her vague, not-terribly-interested tone.

"Yeah."

Lachlyn felt Reame's eyes on her face and she turned, sucked up a smile and returned her attention to the television. Questions she refused to utter bounced around her brain. *Why are you home so early? Did you skip dinner and go straight for dessert? Did you kiss her, flirt with her? God, I'm sure I can smell her perfume...*

"Are you actually watching this?" Reame asked.

"Yeah, it's fascinating," Lachlyn replied.

"Really? Beginner's taxidermy? Are you kidding me?"

Ew! Seriously? Lachlyn focused on the screen where a red-faced, sweating man scraped at an animal skin with a flat blade. Gross. Reame snatched the remote control from her hand, flipped over to a sports channel and held out his hand, bending his fingers into a "give it up" gesture.

"What?" Lachlyn asked, trying for innocence. If

she handed over her bag of chocolates, he'd polish them off in five seconds.

"The candy you are hiding."

Lachlyn widened her eyes and opened her palms. "What candy? I haven't been eating candy."

Reame's thumb swiped her bottom lip and he lifted his thumb to his mouth and sucked. Lachlyn's heart stopped, fell out of her rib cage and flopped onto the floor. Unable to keep her eyes off his, all that gorgeous green, she was caught unaware when Reame's hand shot past her hip to pull the packet from its hiding place. Lachlyn lunged for it but Reame held it up and away from her, his long arms keeping it out of her reach.

"Give it back! That's mine." Lachlyn stood on her knees and reached for the bag, placing her hand on his shoulder to keep her balance as she leaned across his torso to retrieve her chocolate treat.

"C'mon, be nice and share them with me."

"That's my dinner because I didn't eat at one of the city's best restaurants tonight." Lachlyn lunged, toppled and Reame's arm banded around her waist, pulling her close. It felt natural to swing her knee across his lap to straddle him.

Natural but dangerous.

"You had chocolate for dinner?" Reame asked, lowering his arm.

"You don't have much in the fridge and I still don't know what the security procedure is for deliveries. Plus I didn't want to chance it because I heard your high-value client come in."

"Sorry, sweetheart," Reame said, his hand settling on her hip. He seemed quite happy for her to sit on his lap, quite at ease with the fact that her core was resting on his rock-hard erection. She licked her lips. "What did you have for supper?"

Reame's eyes darted to her mouth and back up to her eyes. "Steak, veggies, salad."

She had to ask because they couldn't take this further if he'd so much as kissed his date. "And for dessert?" she whispered.

"Are you asking me if I had sex with my date?"

"I'm asking if anything happened earlier tonight because if it did I'm walking out and going to bed… alone."

Reame's hands tightened on her hips and the packet scratched her skin. "Nothing happened."

"Why not?" Lachlyn whispered.

"Because she wasn't who I wanted." Reame tossed the packet of peanuts onto the couch and reached up to clasp her face. "I thought about it, I admit that. I wanted to burn this crazy I have for you out of my system and I intended to sleep with her. But I couldn't pull the trigger."

Lachlyn lowered her forehead to rest it on his. "I'm glad. I know there are a hundred reasons why we shouldn't but I need to burn the crazy away, too. Maybe when we have we can go back to normal. I can spend some time thinking of whether I want to be a Ballantyne or not—"

"You are a Ballantyne," Reame murmured.

Lachlyn ignored his interruption. "—and you can go back to sleeping with wild women."

That was the plan but she doubted that it would work out that way. But she didn't care. She wanted this, she wanted Reame, she wanted *one* night exploring this fire-hot passion that only he'd ever roused in her. She wanted to know what bliss felt like, whether those Big O's she'd read about were as magical as everybody said they could be if you found a man who knew what he was doing.

Reame, she was convinced, knew what he was doing.

Reame's thumbs caressed her cheekbones, his eyebrows pulled into a slight frown. "You sure about this, Lach?"

Lachlyn shook her head. "No. But I want this. I want you."

Three words—*I want you*—and Lachlyn saw the capitulation in his eyes. Reame moved one hand to the back of her skull and pulled her head down as he reached up to take her mouth in a kiss that was as powerful as it was sensational. Heat, red-hot and fizzing, skittered along her skin, igniting every nerve ending. She wanted to wait, to take this slow, but she couldn't. The sensations he pulled from her were too insistent, too demanding to be ignored. Wrenching her mouth off his, Lachlyn grabbed the hem of her T-shirt with both hands, pulling the cotton up and over her head. She dropped her shirt to the floor and watched Reame's eyes darken as they landed on her chest, her breasts covered by a plain white cotton bra.

She wished she'd worn her prettier lingerie, something far sexier, but judging from Reame's hot gaze, he didn't seem to mind or notice. His big hand easily covered her, his thumb swiping her beaded nub, and Lachlyn groaned, instinctively grinding down on his hard length.

Needing to get her hands on his skin, her fumbling fingers undid the buttons on his shirt and she hastily pushed away the fabric and his jacket, finally connecting with warm, male skin. So different from her own smooth skin, Lachlyn thought, her hand drifting through the light hair on his chest, over flat nipples, down that ridged stomach. She heard Reame's gasp and finally understood the power of being a woman, how good it felt to make a strong, powerful, alpha male groan. And want. And need.

She wanted more, she needed more...now. This was taking far too long and she was scared she'd lose her courage. Lachlyn scooted off his lap, pushed her yoga pants down her legs and stepped out of them, using her toes to push her thick socks off her feet. Damn, but her white cotton briefs and bra would have to go, too. Lachlyn reached behind her back and was about to unsnap her bra when Reame leaned forward, gripped her hips and placed his hot mouth on her stomach, his tongue writing words on her skin. "Sweetheart, slow down."

He didn't understand; she was vibrating with need, terrified that if she stopped, hesitated, that the rush would fade away, that she'd lose the feeling.

Lachlyn wrapped her arms around Reame's head,

pushing her fingers through his silky hair as his fingers danced around her back. With ease, he unhooked her bra and with one finger pulled the garment from her body. Instead of touching her, Reame blew on her nipple, nuzzled the bud with his nose. "You're prettier than I imagined, and I have a damn fine imagination."

"Kiss me, Reame," Lachlyn murmured.

And finally, he did. Reame's tongue curled around her nipple as his other hand cupped her bottom, his fingers running from her ass cheeks down her thighs and inside. Lachlyn opened her legs and felt one finger slide under the band of her panties, perilously close to where she craved his touch.

Lachlyn begged him to touch her, all pretense at pride out of the window. Reame pushed her panties down her thighs and then his fingers were in her cleft, seeking out her point of pleasure. Masculine fingers, knowing fingers, slid inside her as his thumb continued to caress her and Lachlyn felt her orgasm building, felt herself reaching for the impossible. She sucked in her breath and her chest heaved and because she had no words, she guided his mouth back to her nipple and urged him to suck. Pinpoints of pleasure danced behind her eyes, her womb throbbed and she knew she was close, as close as she'd ever been.

But she didn't want her first orgasm to be had alone—this was something she wanted Reame to feel, as well. She wanted him to share in her pleasure, for her to be a part of his.

"Condom?" Lachlyn rasped.

Reame nodded. "Inside pocket of my jacket."

Lachlyn slid her hand under his jacket—he was wearing far too many clothes—and dipped it into his pocket, finding and pulling free a strip of condoms. Ripping one off and apart, she pulled the latex from its wrapper and looked at it, her mind whirling. She shoved it at Reame. "My hands are trembling. You do it."

Reame glanced down at his pants still covering his erection. He moved his fingers inside her and Lachlyn gasped. "I'm a bit busy here. If you want me, you'd better free me."

Lachlyn licked her lips, attacked his belt buckle, opened the button on his jeans and pulled down the zipper. Sucking in her breath, she pushed her fingers under the band of his underwear to encounter him, smooth and oh-so-hard. Lachlyn felt dizzy. He was all male, so much more than she imagined.

And she had a good imagination.

Reame groaned and muttered a low curse. "Scoot." Lachlyn moved away and Reame shot to his feet. He kicked off his boots, removed his socks and dropped his shirt and jacket to the floor. Lachlyn, throbbing, every inch of her skin flushed with heat, sucked in her breath at the sheer perfection of his body. Broad chest—marred only by a scar on the right side of his rib cage—that ridged stomach, strong, muscled legs. And yeah, his beautiful, beautiful—

Reame yanked the condom from her grip, rolled

it down his shaft and reached for her, lifting her up in one arm to walk her around the couch. Turning her to face it, he placed her hands on the back of the couch, his foot nudging her legs apart. Banding his arm around her midsection, he pulled her butt up and caressed her with his free hand, from spine to butt cheeks and between her legs.

So, this wasn't what she was expecting but it was thrilling and exciting.

"You are so damn beautiful," Reame murmured, his mouth dropping to kiss the side of her neck. "I'm going to make you mine now, Lach."

She couldn't wait. Lachlyn felt his head at her entrance, felt the push, felt herself expanding and thought yes, this was what she wanted.

"Relax, baby. You're so damn tight."

Reame's hand sneaked around her hips to play with her bead and Lachlyn liquefied. Instinctively, she pushed backward at the same time Reame surged and she felt a hit of pain before the world exploded behind her eyelids.

Reame stopped in his tracks. "What the hell—"

"Not now, dammit," Lachlyn told him, reaching backward to grip his thighs.

"Lach, I—"

"Not now!" Lachlyn yelled, pushing backward, trying to recapture that intense, supernova feeling. Reame hesitated, cursed her and plunged inside her, hot and hard and melting her from the inside out. Wanting more, wanting everything, Lachlyn tried to touch herself but Reame beat her to it, his fingers finding her, rubbing her as he bucked inside of her. Lachlyn's world exploded into tiny pinpricks of light, her stomach clenched and then she was falling, falling, rolling, touching the universe and everything in it.

From somewhere far away, she heard Reame's shout, felt his body tense and her name being called.

She didn't answer because she was still dancing on the stars.

A little while later, Lachlyn removed her fingernails from Reame's arm and winced at the half moon marks on his skin. She tried to sooth them away, absurdly conscious of Reame's hand between her legs, his shaft still buried deep inside her, the occasional shudder that ran through his body.

Reame touched his lips to her shoulders. "I'm sorry."

"I'm not," Lachlyn told him and it was the truth. For her first time, it had been magical.

"I don't understand," Reame said, keeping his voice low. "You're not a kid so I assumed..."

"Please don't make this a bigger deal than it is, Reame," Lachlyn said, keeping her voice low. "I've had fun with guys but I never dated anyone I liked enough to go this far."

Lachlyn felt Reame tense, heard his sudden intake of breath. "Lach—"

She heard the warning in his voice, the please-don't-read-anything-into-this tone. She patted his arm. "Relax, Reame, I know what this is and it's just sex. I know I'm not the wild woman you wanted but I don't plan to make any demands on you that you can't meet. I don't do personal connections, remember?"

Reame rested his cheek on her shoulder. "That was pretty wild, Lachlyn, for your first time." Reame sounded rueful so Lachlyn pulled away and turned to look at him. She flashed him a cocky grin because he seemed to need the reassurance. "I know, right?"

Reame closed his eyes and shook his head, a small smile touching his lips. Then he sighed. "Your brother is going to kill me."

"So, here's an idea—let's not tell him," Lachlyn suggested.

"He's going to take one look at me and know," Reame said, sounding mournful. "Then he's going to rip my head off."

Lachlyn pushed her hips back and, amazingly, felt him hardening inside her. She thought that men needed some time to recover… "Well, before you die, let's do this again."

Reame's laugh coated her skin in sunshine and she sighed her disappointment when he pulled away from, and out of, her. "Let's clean up and then—" he dropped a kiss on her nose "—we'll do this properly."

"I prefer improperly," Lachlyn said, missing his warmth and touch.

"You are definitely a wild woman in training," Reame said, rueful. "And if your brother doesn't kill me, I suspect you will." He took her hand and led her to his room. "Shower then bed."

Lachlyn stopped in her tracks, tugged her hand from his and ran around the couch to pick up the packet of candy. She waved it at Reame. "I'm still hungry."

"We'll order pizza later." Reame snagged her by the waist and swept her into his arms, laughing when Lachlyn opened the bag of candy and popped one into her mouth. He watched her eat as he walked her into the bathroom. "Are you going to share?" he demanded.

He was trying to act blasé but Lachlyn could see his brain turning, knew that he was trying to work out all the angles. She meant what she'd said earlier; this wasn't a big deal. Well, it was, in the sense that the sex had been utterly delightful, but not in a what-the-hell-have-I-done? way.

"I gave you my virginity, what more do you want?" Lachlyn teased him and was relieved when his mouth quirked up. "Great sex doesn't earn you candy."

"Brat," Reame said as he lowered her to her feet.

Reame shoved his hand into the shower, flipped on the taps and covered her mouth with his. Lachlyn felt him lift her up and then he dropped her under a cold spray of water, snatching the bag out of her hands while she danced around trying to avoid the freezing deluge.

Reame tossed a handful of candy into his mouth before placing the bag on top of the bathroom cabinet, out of her reach, before turning away from her to deal with the condom. Even as she cursed him— using his height was so unfair!—she admired his broad, muscled back, his narrow hips, his truly fantastic butt.

"This water is freezing, Jepsen."

Reame turned back to her, reached past her and flipped on the hot tap. *Right*, Lachlyn thought as hot water poured over her head, her back. She could've done that, too.

Being around Reame fried her brain and judging by the predatory look on his face as he stepped into the shower and pulled her into his arms, he was about to do it again.

She couldn't wait.

# Nine

Finding his bed empty the next morning, Reame pulled on a pair of sweat pants and a ragged sweatshirt and padded out of his bedroom in search of his not-so-reluctant, no-longer-virginal lover. He rubbed his hand over his face, a part of him still not believing that the super-passionate, incredibly lusty woman in his bed was as inexperienced as she could be.

Reame considered feeling guilty about taking her so lustfully and so often but he shrugged that emotion away. Lachlyn was no shrinking violet and had been very vocal in telling him what felt good and what didn't. She was simply a woman who'd waited for a man she liked enough, was deeply attracted to before she allowed him the intimacy of sharing sex with her. And yeah, he felt super-proud that he'd been her first, that she'd taken a chance on him.

Judging by her screaming his name numerous times, he thought he'd done okay.

Reame didn't find Lachlyn in his den or in the kitchen. Booting up his coffee machine, he felt a frigid draft and looked toward the balcony that could be accessed by both bedrooms and the living area, noticing that the sliding door was slightly open. Lachlyn was outside? Holy hell, she had to be freezing. Opening the door, he saw her huddled into a chair in the corner of the balcony, a cashmere blanket wrapped around her tiny body.

"Lach?"

Lachlyn looked up at him and sent him a slow smile. Two strips of blue ran under her eyes and her face looked drawn. They'd spent much of the night making love but he'd dropped off to sleep around 3:00 a.m., Lachlyn in his arms. He was normally a light sleeper and he hadn't heard her rise. "Did you sleep at all last night?"

Lachlyn allowed the blanket to drop and he saw that she'd pulled on his thick parka, her knees tucked up under it. "I'm not a good sleeper."

So that meant no. Pulling up a chair, he faced her and touched her cold cheek with the tips of his fingers. "It's freezing out here. Let's go inside."

Lachlyn ignored that suggestion and he followed her gaze to the familiar ring lying in her palm. He picked up the ring and looked down at the intricate workmanship, his heart bumping off his rib cage. "It's Connor's ring. Linc gave it to you?"

Lachlyn nodded in reply to his question. "He told me what the ring is made from but I can't remember."

Reame ran his fingers over the surface of the ring.

"Bands of Baltic amber and meteorite, separated by thin strips of platinum. I've always loved this ring." He showed her his bare fingers. "I'm not a jewelry-wearing type of guy but this ring kicks ass. I remember him and Sage designing and making it—they cursed the materials and each other for months." He smiled at the memory.

Lachlyn put the big ring onto her thumb and spun it around. "It feels strange that you all have memories of him and I have nothing. I have his blood, his genes, but he's an absolute stranger to me. Then again, so was my mother, for all intents and purposes." Lachlyn tried to smile but he noticed the pain in her eyes, the longing to connect.

Reame took her hand and rubbed his thumb along hers. "Connor was part of my life for a long time. I could answer any questions you have about him."

Lachlyn looked past his shoulder to stare at the cityscape. He waited for her to formulate the words, ignoring the cold wind hammering his back.

"Everyone keeps telling me that, had he known about me, I would've been part of his life," Lachlyn said, her words a whisper on the wind. "Do you think that's true or is that just something they're saying to make me feel better about the situation?"

Reame took his time answering, knowing this was a hard question for her to ask. "I think his actions speak louder than words. Look at what he did for his nephews and niece... As a single guy he took them in after their parents died. From the moment Linc came to live in his house, as the son of his housekeeper, he treated him exactly like he did the other three. He didn't need to adopt the four of them, Lach. He gained nothing legally from that action. He just wanted to tell the world that they were his. So, judging by that, do you honestly think he would've treated you differently?"

Intellectually, he knew that she understood his words but he suspected that she was having a hard time believing them. It had to be really tough, Reame thought, to reconcile the fact that she was Connor's biological daughter and had suffered a hard childhood—mentally, financially and emotionally— while her siblings had had what seemed to be a gilded childhood under the protection of a man who wasn't their real father.

"Are you angry, Lach?"

Judging by the shock that jumped into her eyes, he knew that he'd hit a nerve. "No! Why?"

He placed his other hand on her bare knee and squeezed. "Come on, Lachlyn. Talk to me."

Lachlyn pushed her hair behind her ear and tried to shrink back, pulling her hand from his and moving her knee. Because she was such a fairy, he just needed to tighten his grip slightly to hold her in place. "Are you angry, Lach?" he quietly repeated his question.

Lachlyn's eyes were pure blue fire. "What do you want me to tell you, Reame?"

"The truth."

"The truth?" Lachlyn sprang to her feet, her bare feet hitting the freezing concrete. She didn't seem to notice the cold, that his parka hit her just above her knees and that the sleeves hung a foot over her arms. "Hell, yes, I'm angry! I'm angry that they knew him and I didn't, that they had a parent who loved them enough to make an effort to be a parent. They never had a mother who'd cry herself to sleep or just cry, all the time. I've seen the photos, Reame. They went on family vacations to exotic beaches, went skiing over the Christmas holidays, had piles of presents under the tree, the elaborate birthday parties. Christmas was just another day for us, Reame. Tyce used to draw me pictures for my birthday. I never, once, blew out the candles on a birthday cake! I never sat on my father's lap, had him buy me a pony, got to design rings with him."

He got it now—Sage had lived her life and she was struggling to deal with emotions that idea generated.

"I like Sage, I do!" Lachlyn cried. "She's carrying Tyce's baby, she's going to be my sister-in-law. But it's just…" Lachlyn bit her bottom lip and stared down at her feet, her arms crisscrossed against her body. He couldn't blame her or judge her. She needed to work through her feelings toward Sage, her feelings toward Connor. And he knew that, while she might feel resentful for the life she didn't live, there was something bigger bubbling beneath the surface.

Something she couldn't, or wouldn't, share with him.

He wanted her to. Reame wanted her to spill it, to throw it at his feet so that he could help her bear the load. He wanted to pull her in tight and box away her demons, kick away her pain. Shelter her, protect her.

He was doing it again, he realized. Typical protector behavior, taking on wars that weren't his to fight, situations that didn't need his input. He wasn't anyone's white knight, not anymore. He was trying to get out of the rescue business.

That was why he wanted to date self-confident, independent women, wanted to stay free of emotional entanglements. He didn't want the responsibility of caring for someone else, of fighting their battles, propping them up and making them stronger. It took so much emotional energy.

Lachlyn needed to fight her demons herself and he needed to put some distance between them. Physically and, more crucially, mentally.

This was his time…and he'd messed up by sleeping with her and worse, allowing her to confide in him.

Reame stood up and walked toward the balcony door, gesturing to Lachlyn to come inside. Lachlyn frowned and walked toward him, her expression tight. "Is that your way of saying that this conversation is over and you're tired of hearing me whine?"

Reame rubbed his hand up and down his jaw and thought that honesty now might save some later heartache. "You're not whining but I'm not the person you should be talking to."

Lachlyn stepped into the living room and Reame closed the sliding door behind him.

Lachlyn rocked on her heels, looking ridiculously

young and small in his huge-on-her coat. "You're right. Your loyalty is to Connor and the Ballantynes and you'll always defend them," Lachlyn stated, sounding a hundred years old. "All of you, including Tyce, have picked your sides."

"This isn't about taking sides, Lachlyn. It's not like they are trying to sell you into slavery!" Reame shouted, frustrated. "They are trying to do what's right, what they think is fair."

"What if I don't want what's right, what's fair? What if there is something else I want from them, something else I need?"

"What is that?"

Lachlyn just held his hot stare. "If I have to ask for it then it won't mean as much."

Reame threw his hands up in the hair, intensely frustrated. This was the problem with women. They never just came out and said what they meant, they always had to shade their words. Well, he could teach her to be brutally honest. "Well, they won't know what you want until you tell them." Reame gestured to the bedroom. "I believe in being straightforward, Lachlyn, in laying all my cards on the table."

Lachlyn lifted a challenging eyebrow. "Go on then. Lay your cards on the table, Reame. But if you say anything that sounds patronizing about the fact that I was a virgin, that I am inexperienced, I will throw something at you."

God, he wouldn't insult her like that. She'd chosen not to share her body with anyone but that didn't mean she lacked maturity or independence. Reame hauled in a breath, looking for composure. "Last night you said, before we lost control, that it would be a onetime thing, to blow the crazy away. Do you still stand by that statement?"

*God, say yes. Because if you so much as hint at wanting more, then you'll be back in my arms so fast your head will spin.*

But common sense dictated that they step back and away, that making love again might lead to deeper conversations and that could lead to them feeling more than they should. He didn't want a relationship, he wanted his freedom, to be solely and utterly responsible for himself. Was that too much to ask? Really?

"I think it's better that we chalk last night up to a moment of insanity," Lachlyn said and Reame ignored the jab of disappointment. Lachlyn conjured up a smile. "We scratched an itch and we should leave it at that."

Reame nodded. "I agree with you. It's far simpler that way."

Lachlyn walked toward the guest bedroom and Reame had to fight the urge to run after her, to wind his arms around her tiny waist and kiss her neck, to inhale her perfume. The itch wasn't gone, he admitted. If anything it was bigger and more annoying than before.

Reame lifted his arms up behind his head, laced his fingers, cursed himself and the situation and headed toward his bedroom, wondering how he was going to manage being around her 24/7. Now that he knew how she felt, tasted, the noises she made in the back of her throat when she was turned on, how was he going to be able to keep his hands off her?

All he wanted was a few months free of complications. Anyone would think that he'd asked for world frickin' peace.

The following week, in the basement, Lachlyn boosted herself up onto the steel table in the center of the room and, sitting cross-legged between the piles of paper, opened the small white box next to her. Inhaling the warm, rich scents of caramel and chocolate, she slowly pulled out the cupcake, lifting it to her nose to inhale its sugary wonderfulness.

If Reame knew that she'd left him in the reception area of Ballantyne International and that she'd sneaked out and ran all the way to the bakery two blocks away, he'd be furious.

But traditions were traditions and this was one she'd indulged in all her life. So much had changed in her life but she was determined to hold on to a little of her past.

Lachlyn swiped her finger through the frosting and lifted it to her lips, whimpering when the frosting dissolved on her tongue, spreading sugar and caramel and spice throughout her mouth. Good cupcake, Lachlyn decided. *Happy birthday to me.*

She was twenty-eight today and nobody knew. Well, Tyce should but she doubted that he'd connect this day to her; birthdays hadn't been a big deal in their house. There had been no extra money for gifts and cake and her mom, well, getting through the day was enough of a struggle without having to remember extraneous stuff. As a child she'd heard her school friends talking about birthdays, about parties, gifts and streamers and cake. When she was still living her fantasy of having a family, in her imagination birthdays had been a big deal. There was always a party and she always had a new dress and ribbons threaded through her hair. There were piles of gifts and she was hugged and kissed a lot.

It was always the most perfect day.

Her reality was taking the pennies she managed to scrounge, buying a single cupcake and eating it slowly while the world continued on without her. She'd eaten a hell of a lot of cupcakes alone...

So much had changed, was still in the process of changing. She'd finally had sex, proper sex, with a man whom she liked and it had been everything she'd hoped it would be. She and Sage were talking more. She hadn't seen much of the other Ballantynes lately. Linc was, as far as she knew, still out of town and Jaeger and Beck were busy people. Cady and Piper still sent her the occasional text messages to check in, to remind her that they were free to meet if she wanted company.

She had to admit she was tempted. She'd thoroughly enjoyed talking to Sage over pizza and she imagined that the Ballantyne women were as much fun. Lachlyn put the cupcake down and placed her elbows on her knees. For the first time in over a decade, she allowed her thoughts to drift, for the movie in her head to play.

In the movie, she was racing across Manhattan, late for supper at The Den. The whole family would be waiting for her, either in the upstairs sitting room or in the great room. There would be babies everywhere, Shaw would be on one of his uncles' shoulders and Linc's and Jaeger's toddlers would be tottering around or playing on the jewel-toned Persian carpet. Sage would be on Tyce's lap, his big hands on her belly, and Jaeger and Beck would be arguing about something because that's what they seemed to do. Linc would play peacemaker, handing out wine while Tate put the final touches on supper.

She'd be kissed and hugged hello, handed a glass of wine and someone would ask her about her day, whether she'd found something interesting at work, and she'd feel warm and fuzzy because these were her people, her clan, her soft place to fall.

They'd all turn at the sounds of big boots on the stairs and Reame would step into the room, his eyes quickly moving across the room to find her. Shaw would launch himself at Reame but his eyes would stay on hers, and he'd send her a quick "missed you" smile. She could wait, just, to feel her mouth on his, knowing that she'd have all of him later, for the rest of her life…

*Jesus!* Lachlyn blinked and jerked upright, chills racing up and down her body. She'd had this fantasy before, a large family, a big house, laughter, love. It was like she was twelve again and still believed in the power of dreams.

She didn't. She couldn't.

God, she was losing herself, losing sight of what was important. Her protective shell was cracking and if she didn't rebuild it—if she didn't shore up her defenses—she was going to be annihilated by disappointment. She didn't need the Ballantynes— their money or their company—and she didn't need Reame for sex or companionship. She was fine on her own. She liked being on her own...

Didn't she?

"Pedro's Bakery, Latimore?"

Lachlyn spun around and saw Reame in the doorway wearing a ferocious scowl. "Please tell me that you didn't leave the building to go to a bakery for a cupcake."

Lachlyn glanced down at her half-eaten treat. It wasn't just a cupcake; it was her birthday cupcake. Lachlyn couldn't explain so she just looked at him, noticing that his eyes were a shade warmer than ice. "I am responsible for your safety, Latimore!"

"I went to a bakery, Reame, not to a crack den," Lachlyn protested, lowering her legs and jumping to the floor.

"It's my job to keep you safe and I can't do that if you sneak off behind my back!" Reame shouted. "If you wanted a cupcake, I could've stopped on the way here, or you could've asked me or Linc to organize an intern to run out for one."

But then she would've had to explain why she

wanted a cupcake today, why it was important that she buy it herself. It was her small ritual, a reminder of her independence—a way to remind herself that she could still be alone.

"Your lack of gratitude is astounding. Do you know how much time and effort it takes making sure that you are okay?"

Oh, whoa, hold on a minute. That wasn't fair! "I didn't ask for a bodyguard, that was Linc's idea. You have a company full of guards. I didn't have to become *your* problem. You didn't have to move me into your apartment. That was *your* choice." The apartment she wasn't spending another minute in. Lachlyn slapped her hands on her hips, her temper bubbling. She waved her hands in the air. "You're fired. I release you from all obligations to me. I'm going back to my place—you can deliver my luggage there."

"The hell you will! A child could break into your apartment!"

She should be scared of him. With his wild eyes, clenched fists and heaving chest, he looked the warrior she knew him to be. But she wasn't scared, she was flat-out pissed. Lachlyn closed the gap between them and slapped her open palm on the thin fabric of his blue-and-white-striped shirt. "I am *not* your responsibility. I refuse to be! I can take care of myself. Always have, always will."

Reame grabbed her wrist and yanked her to him, her chest colliding with his. *You are not going to kiss him*, Lachlyn told herself. *You are not going to be a damn cliché.*

"You are the biggest pain in my ass, Latimore. From the moment I heard about you I knew you were going to be trouble."

"Then walk the hell out of my life, Reame. I don't need you, I don't need anybody!" Lachlyn shouted, trying to tug her wrist from his strong grip.

"Keep telling yourself that, honey. Maybe one day you'll actually believe it," Reame growled and then his mouth was on hers. Lachlyn willed herself not to open her mouth, not to let him inside, but it took just one slide of his tongue against the seam of her lips and he was past her first barrier. Determined not to respond, she stood rock still, fighting the battle between temptation and anger. Reame simply gripped her ass and lifted her up to close the distance between them. Holding her with his arm under her butt, he used his other hand to hold the back of her head, tilting it so that he had better access to her mouth.

"Kiss me, dammit." Reame muttered the words against her mouth and Lachlyn heard the rasp in his voice, the need below his rough command. If she was a better woman she'd stick to her guns, keep herself aloof, but this was Reame and he was kissing her, slowly liquefying her joints. Lachlyn wound her arms around his neck and pushed her tongue into his mouth, wanting to do her own tasting and feasting.

She could taste the coffee he'd had earlier, and the fresh tang of his toothpaste. His hair was silky soft under her fingers and the bone-hard erection pushing into her stomach. He felt like heaven with undercurrents of sin. Hot hands pulled her legs apart and she obeyed his silent request to wind them around his waist. Then his erection was rubbing against her core and she could feel his heat and steel through his suit pants and her leggings. His hand worked its way under her thigh-length sweater, covering most of her lower back as he pushed her closer to him.

He just had to keep rocking into her and she'd spin off on a band of pleasure. Just a little more, she thought, grinding against him, a harder kiss, another rock...

Lachlyn felt her butt hit the table and, *nonono*, he wrenched his mouth off hers. Lachlyn reached for him, but Reame threw his hands up in a *just stop* gesture. He bent over, placing his palms on his thighs, and stared at the floor.

"I don't need this in my life," Reame muttered, his words poison-tipped bullets spinning through her heart. Of course he didn't need her. She was extraneous, a distraction, a burden. She was, as he'd stated, a pain in the ass.

Reame stood up and pointed a finger at her, his expression a weird combination of pissed-off male and turned-on male. "I will be back at five to pick you up and take you home. Do not make me look for you, Lachlyn."

She couldn't stay with him. She refused to inconvenience him any more than she already had. "I'll make other arrangements, Reame. I refuse to be a burden and I am not your responsibility!"

Reame gripped her face with one hand. "Five o'clock, Latimore. Be here."

Reame spun around and weaved his way through boxes to the door. Lachlyn looked down and picked up the box holding the cupcake. Dropping down from the table, she walked to the trash bin and tossed the box inside.

*She'd had a couple of crappy birthdays before but this one, excuse the expression, took the cake.*

Reame's foul mood hadn't dissipated by the time he got back to his desk. Slamming his office door closed, he flung himself into his chair and stared at his blank monitor. He wasn't sure what he was more pissed about, the fact that Lachlyn went AWOL on her own or that she thought that she wasn't worth his time and effort.

Why couldn't she see her worth? Why was she so convinced that she had nothing to give? She was super-smart and, when she allowed herself to relax, surprisingly funny. The other night, after he returned to his apartment with Tyce, he'd listened to her talk with her brother and Sage. Either the wine had made her tongue loose or she was finally starting to feel comfortable with Sage, but she'd shown no signs of the loner she professed herself to be. She was a lively conversationalist and, surprisingly, quite affection- ate. She'd touched Sage's arm to make a point, rested her head against Tyce's shoulder, kissed and hugged them both goodbye. He'd had a glimpse of the real Lachlyn and, crappit, he really liked her.

He also really liked her body. She was small, sure, but perfectly formed, feminine from the top of her head to that silver-ringed toe. Knowing that she was just down the hallway half-naked and that he couldn't touch her was a special type of hell. The biggest problem with Lachlyn was that she was the first woman in a long time that he could imagine dating, spending long periods of time with. He liked her steel-trap mind. Her laughter made his stomach flip. Her vulnerability made him want to slay her dragons.

She was exactly what he wasn't looking for. He was out of the business of slaying dragons, running to the rescue. While he never expected anyone to fight his battles, he just didn't want to take on another person's drama. And Lachlyn had more than most. No, he was sticking to his plan…he wanted to have uncomplicated sex with uncomplicated women.

*You use the word* want *a lot. Why don't you just do it?*

Lachlyn's words popped into his head and ricocheted through his brain. She was right—he'd been talking big but hadn't put any of his words into action. Truthfully, he only wanted to sleep with Lachlyn again, and again, but she was firmly off-limits. What the hell had he been thinking earlier, kissing her like that?

Her skin was like satin and he loved the sounds she made in the back of her throat when she was turned on. And the way she slid her core up and over him…he'd come close to losing his load right there and then. Reame rubbed his hands over his face. *Stop thinking about Lachlyn, moron, and get your head in the game.*

Lachlyn, for a hundred and one reasons—the best being that she was Linc's sister, inexperienced and too damn vulnerable—was off-limits. He wasn't going to sleep with her again. In fact, it was better if he did put some distance between them, find her another place to stay. Truthfully, the attention around her had died down and he thought it was reasonably safe for her to go back to her apartment. He could easily arrange for one of his agents to escort her to work and back. There was no reason for her to stay in his apartment except that he liked having her there.

He didn't like that he liked having her there. It felt too much like something real, something similar to the relationships the Ballantynes were enjoying. He was happy that his friends were happy but fairy tales didn't last forever. He should know—he'd watched his parents' marriage detonate without rhyme or reason. Love didn't last, and the country's divorce statistics proved his case. And if it didn't last then what was the point of even trying? And what if he messed it up? What if he failed?

The rewards, companionship and sex, weren't worth the risk and failure was never an option. Sex was easy to find and he had good friends who kept him entertained. So he'd stick to the plan.

Reame pulled his phone out of his suit jacket and scrolled through his dating app. He chose and then dismissed a dozen women before cursing himself. This should not be that difficult. These were smart, nice, hot women who were on the same sex-only page. Reame stared down at a brunette, trying to make sense of her profile. Professional, intelligent, not looking for anything permanent. Perfect. He swiped right and because she'd already indicated that she was interested, sent her a message suggesting drinks. She suggested dinner and Reame agreed.

See, what was so hard about that? Nothing really, if he ignored the acid-inducing feeling that he was cheating on Lachlyn.

Cora rapped on his door and, grateful for the distraction, Reame called for her to come in. She held a cup of coffee in one hand and a stack of files in the other. "Is it safe to come inside?"

Reame sent her a sour look as she placed his cup of coffee next to his elbow. "Thanks. Can you make a reservation for me for dinner for two tonight? Someplace nice."

"Sure. Glory's make a fuss of ladies on their birthday, they make this wonderful cocktail which you can only order if it's your birthday."

What the hell was Cora talking about? "Why are you going on about birthdays?" Reame demanded, flipping through the files. More expenses, staff rotations, background checks. Staff reviews. The fun never ended...

Cora looked puzzled. "I presumed that you were taking Lachlyn to dinner because it's her birthday."

Reame's stomach felt as heavy as a boulder. *Please tell me that you are joking*, he silently begged Cora. But he knew that he was out of luck. That explained the cupcake. Her solitary celebration cracked his heart.

*I never, once, blew out the candles on a birthday cake.*

Reame dropped the folders, feeling sick to his stomach. Reame was damn sure that nobody, not even her brother, remembered that it was her birthday. He'd had his a few months back and his mom and sisters all called him before he'd had a chance to wipe the sleep from his eyes. Throughout that morning he'd taken calls from every Ballantyne who could speak on a telephone. Cora ordered pizza for lunch and he'd eaten with his staff in the break room. That evening, he and the Ballantyne men had hit a couple bars for an evening of beer and pool.

It had been a great day.

Lachlyn had bought herself a cupcake. And he'd chastised her for it. Reame shuddered and held his head in his hands.

Lachlyn pressed her cheek to Tyce's heart and closed her eyes. Her big brother bent his knees and tightened his arms around her. It was the best hug she'd ever received from him and a great way to end what she was sure was the best evening of her life.

"Sorry I forgot, Lach," Tyce muttered and she heard the regret in his voice. It was past eleven and they were standing at the entrance to the basement of the Ballantyne building. The rest of the family had left and Reame and Sage were standing by the elevator giving her and her brother time to talk.

Lachlyn dropped her head back to look up at him. "It's fine, Tyce. We were never good at birthdays."

Tyce tucked a strand of hair behind her ear. "And I'm also sorry for that."

Lachlyn blinked away her tears. "You were trying to keep us fed, keep a roof over our heads, while still going to school. There is no blame, big brother, only gratitude that you were there."

Tyce kissed her forehead before cupping her face in her hands. "You have an opportunity to change your life, baby girl."

"It's too much money, Tyce."

"We're not talking about the money, Lach, and you know it. I'm talking about giving yourself a chance to love this family. To love a man."

Lachlyn shook her head, instantly in denial. "He doesn't want a relationship and neither do I. He's just looking after me because Linc asked him to."

"Oh, BS, Lachlyn! He has a hundred employees. He could've asked any one of them to guard you. He moved you into his apartment when he could've put you into a hotel. He organized a last-minute surprise birthday party, threatening death if we didn't cancel whatever plans we had this evening and get our butts down here to this basement."

Lachlyn looked behind her and saw her steel table covered with a pretty tablecloth, takeout containers scattered across its surface. Empty bottles of wine sat on the floor and the wingback chair was piled high with presents. Nothing terribly expensive, just thoughtful gifts from thoughtful people.

Reame hadn't given her a present but organizing this party was the best gift he could've given her. All four Ballantynes and their partners attended her ad hoc party, plus Linc's mom, Jo, and Linc's PA Amy and her wife. They'd all walked into the basement shortly after six, carrying wine and takeout, presents, dropping birthday kisses on her cheek.

"Tonight I felt like I was part of the family," Lachlyn admitted, picking a piece of lint from Tyce's shirt.

"Honey, you *are* part of the family. The only person who doesn't realize it is you," Tyce told her. "This was what you wanted, Lachlyn. All your life you've wanted this. It's yours for the taking. *Take it.*"

"I'm scared, Tyce."

"I know, Lachlyn. I was scared, too. I get it, I do. It's so much easier being alone but it's also so damn selfish and far *too* easy." Tyce held her hand between both of his, his dark eyes filled with emotion. "Mom, she was selfish, Lach. She liked being depressed. She enjoyed being useless—"

Lachlyn tried to tug her hand away but he held tight. "Don't say that. She was sick!"

"Sure, but she had options to get better. Taking her damn antidepressants would've helped but she chose not to, Lachlyn. She chose to check out, because getting better, interacting, loving us meant work, hard work. It was easier to hide, to sleep, to fade away. By not raising us, she made us selfish, Lach. She made it seem okay to hide, to not try." Tyce squeezed her fingers. "You've got to *try*, Lach."

"I just wanted her to love me, Tyce," Lachlyn said,

the tears that had been so close to the surface all evening finally released and rolling down her face.

"And the fact she couldn't was her problem, not yours. No one, except Mom apparently, gets out of this life without having dirty knees and a broken heart. When are you going to break up with your childhood, Lach? When are you going to release its hold on you? Because no matter how independent you are you still need, and deserve, to be taken care of sometimes. This family, and Reame, seem to want to do that."

"Tyce, you ready to go?" Sage called from down the hall.

"Yeah, on my way." Tyce gave her another long hug and when he stepped away, Lachlyn looked at Sage who blew her a kiss. Then her eyes slammed into Reame's and Lachlyn barely registered her brother and Sage's last goodbyes.

Reame stalked over to her and clasped her face in his hands. "Happy birthday, honey. I'm sorry for earlier."

Lachlyn's fingers encircled his wrists and her heart stumbled and sighed. "Thank you for my fabulous birthday party. Best gift *ever*."

Reame dropped his hand and led her back into the messy room. "Linc asked me to tell you that he instructed the night supervisor to send the cleaning crew down in thirty minutes to clean up after us."

"I was going to do it," Lachlyn protested, picking up a container containing a lone slice of pizza. She started to pile the Chinese takeout containers on top, jamming paper napkins into the containers. She wasn't sure what to say, or how to act. Earlier today she and Reame had been yelling at each other and she was pretty sure she'd fired him at one point. But, despite the ugly words they'd exchanged, he'd organized a surprise party for her.

She was both touched and confused.

Where was she going to sleep tonight? Back at Reame's place or in her own apartment? Would he take her to work in the morning or would she have to go back to using public transportation?

Lachlyn suddenly felt exhausted and oh so emotional—although her conversation with her brother about their mother had been brief, it had been intense. She wanted time to think, to mull over Tyce's words, to take them apart and examine them. Lachlyn jammed the boxes into the trash bin and looked up to see Reame propping his phone against a pizza box. A haunting melody filled the room.

Reame held out his hand, his eyes on her face. A small smile touched his lips. "We have half an hour... Dance with me?"

Lachlyn placed her hand in his, her soul sighing when she stepped into his embrace, his big hand between her shoulder blades. His chin rested on her temple as he moved her in a slow circle around the room.

"I didn't buy you a present." Reame's words rumbled across her temple, down her neck.

"I don't need a present, Reame. I had this wonderful evening and you're dancing with me."

Reame tightened his grip on her and she heard his sharp intake of breath. "I don't want to hurt you, Lach. I can't give you what you need."

Lachlyn brushed her thumb against the cord in his neck and felt him shudder. "I'm still figuring out what I need, Ree. Will you take me home? Can you give me tonight?"

Reame's lips moved against her hair and his hand pulled her closer to him so that there was only a paper-thin gap between them. "Yeah."

"Then let's take tonight and tomorrow can take care of itself."

# Ten

"The brothers are getting restless."

Sage was sitting on one of the three steel tables in the cavernous storeroom, sandwiched between piles of Ballantyne documents and photographs dating from the 1920s and 1930s. Since her impromptu birthday party ten days ago, the Ballantynes and their partners had taken to popping down to the basement on odd occasions but Sage was her most frequent, almost daily visitor. On the days she didn't see Sage's lovely face, Lachlyn felt cheated. Sage wasn't only the love of her brother's life, she was fast becoming her closest friend.

So much for keeping her distance…

Lachlyn, digging into a box, pulled out another leather-bound diary and, seeing the initials on the cover, frowned. "How did your great-grandmother's diary from 1928 end up in a box holding mostly correspondence from the 1950s?" Lachlyn demanded, frustrated. "The Ballantyne filing system is appalling, Sage!"

"So you've told me, a time or twenty," Sage replied before biting into her half-eaten apple. "Are you ignoring my comment about my brothers?"

*I'm trying to*, Lachlyn silently admitted.

"None of us understand why you are hesitating, Lachlyn. And the brothers want a decision by the end of the month. That's in ten days."

"I have ten days to decide?"

"No, you have a week. We need some time to tell the accountant what we plan to do so he can factor in—" Sage wrinkled her nose "—what needs to be factored in."

Like Lachlyn, Sage did not have a head for numbers. "I don't know if I can make a decision by then," Lachlyn said, carefully placing the diary with the others she'd found.

"You're going to have to, Lach," Sage said, hopping off the table and holding her stomach with one hand. The sound of the heavy door opening interrupted their conversation and Lachlyn spun around, eager to welcome anyone into her basement space, particularly if that person wasn't a Ballantyne and wouldn't talk about her becoming one in name and money.

It was Reame. Lachlyn glanced at her watch and saw that it was past quitting time and Reame was late to collect her. She hadn't noticed because she'd been so fascinated by the history in this room. Not only was she getting a thorough education on all things

Ballantyne, she'd also discovered various items and documents that allowed her a glimpse into how the city had changed over the past hundred and twenty years, and how norms and culture had altered. This history should be collated, recorded and shared with the world.

Lachlyn pulled her attention back to her brother's fiancée. Sage patted Reame's big arm as she passed him on her way to the door. "Try to talk some sense into her about taking our offer, Ree."

Reame nodded, shut the door after Sage left and immediately walked over to the stuffed chair in the corner of the room, sinking into it like he'd been awake for days. "Hey."

"Hey back," Lachlyn said, remaining by the steel table, her hand on a tower of black-and-white photographs. "You're late."

Reame didn't reply, he just tipped his head back and stared up at the unpainted ceiling. Lachlyn did a tip-to-toe scan, starting at his expensive shoes, up his muscled legs covered by gray suit pants. He wore a white, open-collared shirt and a jacket matching his pants. One end of his pale blue tie peeked out from his suit pocket.

His shoulders were hunched halfway up to his ears and his jaw was rock-hard with tension. Lachlyn opened her mouth to ask him what was wrong but bit back the words. It wasn't the time. She recognized his need for quiet, to be alone with his thoughts and to work through whatever was tying him up in knots. Reame was even more spooked by relationships than she was, so they were trying to keep things uncomplicated, making love but avoiding conversation that dipped below the surface of politeness.

Since Reame didn't want to talk, Lachlyn turned back to the box she'd been making her way through, rapidly sorting through the paperwork previous Ballantynes had left her to find. Lachlyn picked up a bundle of letters secured with a silk ribbon and pulled one from the bundle, opening it up with gentle fingers.

February 1926,
My darling Matthew…
It is snowing again and I am bereft without you…

Lachlyn read three letters before Reame pulled her back into the present by standing up and walking over to the tiny bar fridge in the corner and pulling out a water. He slammed the door shut, cracked the top and took a long pull, draining half of the bottle within a matter of seconds.

He looked exhausted and so very alone. If there was ever an emotion she could easily recognize, it was loneliness. How best to get him to open up, she wondered, carefully folding one of the letters. She hated it when people prodded and probed, bugged her to talk, so she kept her statement short. "If you want to talk, I'll listen."

Reame stared at his feet, finished his water and crumpled the plastic bottle in his hand. "I had a craptastic day," he admitted, his low voice drifting over to her.

"It happens," Lachlyn stated, knowing that Reame wouldn't appreciate sympathy. Narrowing her eyes, she looked around for a particular box.

Lachlyn zeroed in on the box and, pulling a box cutter from her back pocket, sliced open the tape. Inside were six bottles of ten-year-old whiskey that she knew were a Christmas gift from a Scottish laird to Connor.

Since nobody but she knew the box was here and thinking that Connor wouldn't mind her filching a bottle, she pulled one out and, walking back to Reame, cracked the seal and removed the top. She held it out to him and smiled at his grateful look.

"I can find you a cup if you want one," Lachlyn said as his fingers wrapped around the neck of the bottle.

Reame snorted his refusal. "Please." He took a hit and then another one before offering her the bottle. "This was Connor's favorite whiskey. He got a couple of cases delivered every few months."

Lachlyn refused his offer and looked around. "I can't believe what I am finding in this storeroom, and that is one of the less weird items."

Folding her arms, she looked up at Reame and saw that the whiskey had chased a little of his anger away. "So, why did you have a—what did you call it?—craptastic day?"

Reame took her hand and pulled her onto his lap,

one hand on her thigh and the other still holding the bottle of whiskey.

"My mother left today on a cruise. As she was preparing to board, she realized that she forgot her passport and ticket on the kitchen counter. She lives in South Orange," Reame said, placing the bottle on the floor.

"Nice," Lachlyn said, thinking of the New Jersey neighborhood, with its quaint houses and gaslight-lined streets.

"I wanted to send Cora but no, I had to go because she doesn't want strangers in her house. Cora has worked for me for five years and has met my mother twenty-plus times. So I belted out to South Orange, picked up the documents, eventually found her at the cruise ship terminal, where I listened to her twenty-minute monologue about why this trip wasn't a good idea before making my escape."

Lachlyn ducked her head, trying to hide her smile. Under his irritation she heard his affection for his mother in his voice. "As I hit the office, I receive a message from my younger sister, Lara, telling me that she hates her job and has resigned. She's now jobless and homeless and doesn't think accounting is for her."

"Do you want me to move out of your place so your sister can move into your second bedroom?"

Reame looked horrified. "Hell, no! But could she not have decided this earlier and saved me a crap-load of college fees?"

"You paid for her education?"

"Somebody had to," Reame snapped. "I have three younger sisters and when the oldest got to senior year, my dad walked out on his twenty-five-year marriage, cleaned out all his bank accounts and bailed."

Lachlyn saw pain and disappointment wash across Reame's face. "What happened then?"

"I was twenty-five, in the military and loving my life. Yeah, war was hard and the tours were tough. We were an elite unit and the pressure was intense. I made life-or-death decisions on a daily basis, but I believed in what we were doing and I believed in my men. We were tight.

"My mom told me what happened and said that she couldn't cope. She had no money and my sisters, ages fifteen to seventeen, were beside themselves. I had to go home. When I got Stateside, my mom was a walking zombie and my sisters were all acting up in different ways. One was studying herself to death, another was sneaking out at night, the youngest was all but living at her boyfriend's house. I couldn't go back to my unit. They needed me."

"Then Connor stepped in," Lachlyn guessed.

"Yeah. He gave me a job as his bodyguard, then as his head of security. Then he suggested that I go out on my own. He provided the capital I needed, and between the business profits and student loans, my sisters all got a decent education."

"And your mom?"

"She found a job and between her salary and me helping out, she got back on her feet. Emotionally, she never recovered. She thought she had this perfect marriage, that everything was amazing between her and my dad, she just never saw him for who he really was."

"Who was he, Reame?"

"An intensely selfish man who felt confined by his circumstance, by marriage, by the kids who demanded time and money and attention from him."

Lachlyn toed off her sneakers and tucked her feet beneath her, curling up in his lap. "What else happened today, Reame?"

Reame lifted an eyebrow. "That isn't enough?"

"You're a Special Forces soldier, and while your sister's actions are annoying and having to retrieve your mom's documents was irritating, that wasn't enough to put you in such a foul mood."

"We moved the high-value target out of the guest suite and into his safe house today. He and my guys were ambushed on route because my client leaked his whereabouts to his mistress," Reame stated quietly, fury coating every word. "I was supposed to be riding along but I asked Liam to go along instead of me, because I was chasing down my mother's missing passport. A passing car opened fire on them."

"Was anybody hurt?" Lachlyn asked, dreading the answer.

Reame shook his head. "No and the client is fine." There was no blood left in Reame's clenched fists. "It could've ended badly, Lachlyn. Really badly. All because he couldn't keep his mouth shut."

Lachlyn rolled the fat body of the whiskey bottle between her palms. "What a moron."

"Tell me about it. He put my guys at risk so I terminated his contract." Reame tipped his head back to look at the ceiling. "I am just so sick of responsibility, Lach. Liam has a wife, kids. If he was killed, I don't think I could live with myself."

Lachlyn looked at him and saw stress—the tension in his arms, his tired eyes, the grooves down the side of his mouth so much deeper than normal. His fantastic eyes were a flat green, almost as if they were too tired to show emotion. People entrusted their property and lives to him and his men and he, as head of Jepsen & Associates, was ultimately responsible for every life, every business, every piece of property. That was a hell of a load to carry.

"Do you ever feel like you want to throw up your arms and lie down and be taken care of? Just once?"

Reame rolled his head to look at her, his eyes speculative. "Yeah. I sometimes wish that someone would step in and make some decisions, *any* decision."

So not the tough-guy, I-can-handle-it response she'd expected. Well, then, she might be able to help him out. "Being an adult sucks," Lachlyn murmured before standing up and moving to the door. She twisted the lock closed, effectively locking them into the storeroom. She could do this, she thought. She could make the first move. She'd lead and God, she hoped he'd follow.

Lachlyn played with the buttons of her shirt as

she made her way back to Reame, fighting the urge to bite her lip. *You have to look at him, Latimore. This can't happen without eye contact.*

"What are you doing, Lach?" Reame's voice was a low rumble.

"Making a decision for you," Lachlyn said, her fingers working the buttons on her shirt. "Taking care of you."

"I thought we were keeping this on the surface, keeping it simple."

Lachlyn shrugged out of her shirt, her eyes on his. She flushed as she stood in front of him in her rose-pink bra, her skin pebbling with anticipation. "Shh, that sounds like you are thinking. Don't think, just feel. Step out of your life, your head and let me love you," Lachlyn said, straddling his legs and placing her hands on his shoulders.

"Lach, do you think this is a good idea?" Reame demanded as his big hands settled on her waist, his thumb swiping her skin.

"It's not your decision but mine. You don't have to think, or run options or scenarios… You just have to enjoy." Lachlyn placed her hands on his cheeks, enjoying his stubble under her hands. He smelled of mint and whiskey, like a turned-on man. "Let me do all the work—consider this my gift to you."

Reame's eyes drilled into hers and she could see him fighting temptation. Lachlyn dropped her head and her mouth drifted over him. "Let me give you this, Reame. Please? Relax, enjoy."

"It's a dusty storeroom in the bowels of the Ballantyne building," Reame protested.

"The door is locked." Lachlyn curved her lips against his. "We have a chair and I know that you have a condom in your wallet. Stop thinking, Reame. Let go."

"Lach—"

Lachlyn saw the capitulation in his eyes and her mouth dropped onto his, her lips playing with his, exploring, tasting, feasting. She sensed him losing control, knew that he was on the verge of taking charge of this encounter, so she pulled back and picked his hands off her waist and placed them on the arms of the chair. "This is about you, not me," Lachlyn told him. "Keep your hands there."

"I don't think I can," Reame said, his voice hoarse.

"You can," Lachlyn replied. "Let me play, Reame."

Reame groaned, dropped his head back and closed his eyes, and Lachlyn knew that she'd won this battle. Knowing that Reame was naturally impatient, she kissed him again, tracing her tongue over his bottom lip, nibbling her way up his jaw, nuzzling her nose into that delicious space between his jaw and neck. She sucked, gently, before soothing the skin with a tiny lick. She heard his low, masculine rumble of appreciation and her soul smiled. Lachlyn kissed her way across his collarbone, her hands on his chest, conscious of his elevated heart rate. It made her feel strong and powerful, so intensely feminine, that such a man—an alpha to his core—wanted her, burned for her. For *her*, inexperienced and unknowing, but so, so willing to learn. Lachlyn fumbled with the buttons of his shirt, sighing when she pulled the sides apart to reveal his muscled chest.

"I'm so glad my first time was with you," Lachlyn murmured, her fingers dancing across his flat nipples, her eyes locked on his. "Thank you for letting me do this, for letting me touch you."

Reame's eyes flared with passion and he licked his lips. "That's never a problem, sweetheart. But I have to say, you are driving me crazy. Not being able to touch you is both hell and heaven."

Lachlyn was content to look at him, her fingers skating across his ridged stomach, across the top of his hard thighs. She looked down and saw his erection straining the fabric of his suit pants. She lifted hot, heavy eyes. "That looks uncomfortable," Lachlyn said, sounding a little wicked.

"You have no damn idea," Reame retorted. "Can I touch you yet?"

Lachlyn shook her head. "I'm not done exploring." Lachlyn scooted off his lap and bent down to pull off his shoes, then his socks. Standing up, she leaned over him, her blond hair falling into his face. She tucked it behind her ear as her hands went for his belt buckle. Reame protested but she cut off his words with a kiss, pushing her tongue into his mouth to tangle with his. He was as into the kiss as she was. She could feel the passion rumbling beneath his control as he allowed her to take the lead, as she advanced and retreated. His trust in her both warmed and emboldened her, and her hands steadied as she flipped open his belt and unhooked the snap on his suit pants. Now owning her confidence, she placed her palm on his erection, sighing at the evidence of his desire.

For her. Only for her.

Reame cursed, then sighed. "Get naked," he muttered.

Lachlyn raised a sassy eyebrow. "Uh, my show, remember? This is about you, not me."

Reame frowned, uncomfortable. "I can't do this unless you are with me, Lach, every step of the way. That's not the way this works."

So honorable, Lachlyn thought. And that was the problem. Reame had no idea that he could occasionally put his needs first. He had no concept of how to take, only how to give. "Right now, this is exactly how it works."

Through the soft cotton of his underwear, Lachlyn stroked him, rubbing her thumb over his tip, feeling him shudder, jump, with every touch. She wanted to kiss him, to lose herself in his mouth, desperate for his hands between her legs, but she knew that if she did, she'd lose him, lose control of the situation.

"Where's that condom, Ree?"

"Inside jacket pocket. Wallet," Reame said, his eyes glazed with passion.

"Get it," Lachlyn ordered.

While Reame fumbled through his wallet, Lachlyn, still dressed, pushed her hands beneath his underwear and suit pants, urging him to lift his butt.

Pulling his pants off him, she stood back to look at him and sighed. Reame looked magnificent in just an open jacket and shirt. "Man, you're hot," Lachlyn told him, her eyes traveling up his muscled legs, over his impressive groin, that wide chest and to that face that stopped traffic. "I want you so much."

Reame had the condom halfway to his mouth and his eyes flew to hers, pure green fire. Three words—*I want you*—were enough to push him over the edge, to snap his control. Letting out a muted roar, his arms shot out and wrapped around her waist, pulling her onto him. He stood up, holding her with one arm as he ripped the packet open with his teeth. Thrusting the condom into her hand, Reame lowered her to her feet, his mouth hot on hers as he shrugged out of his shirt and jacket.

"What are you doing?" Lachlyn asked, her voice trembling, as he expertly flicked open the button to her jeans. He then sneaked his hands down the back of her jeans, underneath her panties, and Lachlyn felt cool air on her butt and thighs as the material fell to the floor. "I was going to make love to you!"

"Yeah, well, crap happens," Reame retorted, before unsnapping her bra and pulling her naked chest flush against his. He clasped her face in both his hands, dropping hot, open-mouth kisses on her cheekbone. "I can't stand not being able to touch you. I need to touch you."

Lachlyn closed her eyes as his sexy words sent her already high internal temperature rocketing.

"That condom on yet?" Reame asked against her mouth.

"No space to work." Lachlyn managed to find and utter the words, a minor miracle because she'd lost all power to her brain. Her hands were trapped between their bodies so Reame moved backward. While Reame traced the shell of her ear with his tongue and lips—man, that felt amazing—Lachlyn fumbled with the condom, her hands shaking.

Reame placed his hands on hers and together they rolled the condom over his hard, hot skin. Reame showed her how to touch him, how to roll him in her hand. And the more she touched him, the hotter she got, her own need for him clawing at her from the inside out.

"I can't take much more," Reame told her, his voice low and guttural. "You ready for me, baby?"

Lachlyn managed a low "Yes."

"Think I better check," Reame teased and slid his fingers between her legs, and Lachlyn sucked in her breath at his desperate groan.

Reame rested his forehead on hers, his breath shallow. "So hot, so wet." Lachlyn felt all the air leave the room so she did the only thing she could think of—she kissed him. He was all she needed.

Reame inhaled her, sucked her inside him and Lachlyn felt herself falling, whirling. Boosting her up his body, her legs encircled his waist and then Reame was inside of her, filling her, making her whole.

Walking her backward, he somehow managed to

find a steel table and not even the cold metal against her backside managed to shock her out of her Reame-induced stupor. Nothing else existed but Reame's touch, his smell, his tongue in her mouth and his hands on her hips as he poured himself into her.

"Need you, need you, need you," Reame chanted in her ear.

Lachlyn, unable to speak, arched into him, tightening her legs around his waist as he took her on a roller coaster ride of passion.

He pushed into her, she sighed, he pushed again, she cried out. Passion built and built, pulling her up to where nothing mattered but this, him, the world they'd created together.

"Now, Lach, dammit. Do it," Reame ordered her, his voice harsh in her ear.

Lachlyn splintered into bright, jewel bright shards as she dimly felt Ream's tension, his utterly still body, before he shattered in her arms. Slowly, so slowly, her mind started to stitch itself back together again and she became aware of Reame's heavy breathing, his weight, the cold table beneath her skin, the fact that he'd swept piles of carefully sorted papers onto the floor.

It didn't matter, nothing mattered. Reame was holding her, and as long as he did—like she was the most precious mineral in the world—she was content.

Maybe even happy.

# Eleven

Lachlyn looked up at the sound of footsteps, thinking Reame had returned to collect her. After making love, he'd told her that he'd take her home but first he had to meet a client for a drink and that he hoped it wouldn't be a late night. Feeling wired from their lovemaking and not wanting to sit in an empty apartment by herself—wow, first time she'd felt that—Lachlyn told him she preferred to work in the basement. He could collect her later but he'd better bring her some food.

Making love made her hungry.

But, sadly, it wasn't Reame with food but one of the nighttime cleaning staff, pulling her cart. She sent Lachlyn a tentative smile and softly asked whether it would be a good time to clean.

Lachlyn waved her in, thinking that her mom, nearly thirty years ago, might've worn that same green-and-blue uniform, worked these same hours.

On the tag clipped to the woman's uniform Lachlyn saw the name Greta. The cleaner coughed and with her red nose and bright eyes, looked like she might be fighting the flu. She was probably at work because she had children to feed, rent to pay.

Lachlyn walked over to her, placed her hand on her cart and nodded to the wingback chair. "Why don't you sit down for five minutes? You look like you could use the break."

Greta shook her head so hard that her gray streaked bun threatened to fall apart. "I can't. I have work to do, a schedule to follow."

"How long are you allocated to clean in here?"

Greta sent a longing look at her chair before sending a quick look at her watch. "Thirty minutes."

"Then you can sit down for thirty minutes," Lachlyn insisted. "My work area was cleaned last night—it doesn't need to be done again."

"I don't think—"

For the first, and most likely the last, time Lachlyn pulled rank. "I'm a Ballantyne, Greta, and I say you should."

Surprised gratitude flashed across her face and the tiny woman sank into her chair, closing her eyes in relief. She really wasn't well, Lachlyn thought. Walking over to her makeshift kitchen—coffeepot, kettle and microwave—she poured Greta a cup of coffee. Asking how she preferred it, she added the last of her cream and two sugars, hoping that the sugar would give the older woman an energy boost.

"Are you sick?" Lachlyn asked, pushing the cup into her shaking hands.

"A persistent cold," Greta replied, before lifting the cup to her mouth.

Lachlyn hooked a small wooden stool with her foot and sat down in front of Greta, noticing a fine sheen of perspiration on her brow. That wasn't good, Lachlyn thought; it looked like she was running a temperature.

Greta looked sick and miserable and, worst of all, uncomfortable with being waited on by a Ballantyne, so Lachlyn attempted to put her at ease. "My mother was a night cleaner, in this very building," Lachlyn said softly. "That's how she met Connor Ballantyne."

Greta's thick eyebrows lifted. "I thought that was fake news, something the newspapers wrote to sell papers."

"No, it's true. She worked here for a few years and she used to clean Connor's office."

Greta rested her cup on her knee, her faded blue eyes thoughtful. "I can't believe Mr. Connor has been gone for nearly four years now. Before he got sick, he was often in the building late at night. He was a friendly man who talked to everyone. He was larger than life, happy, you know?"

Unfortunately, she didn't, but Lachlyn smiled anyway.

"He didn't like quiet. We always knew when Mr. Connor was working late because he'd play his stereo very loud or he'd sing. Sometimes both at the same time. He couldn't hold a tune."

Lachlyn grinned at the image. She leaned forward as if to impart a great secret. "Neither can I."

"I'm sorry you never met him." Greta tapped her finger against her mug. "But your mother would've told you about him."

That was a reasonable assumption but...no.

"Your mother should be very proud of you, Miss Lachlyn."

It was such a simple statement but it rocked her to her core. Feeling off balance, Lachlyn stood up, told Greta to rest, walked back to her steel table and lifted the photograph she'd been examining before Greta had arrived. The image refused to come into focus.

She'd spent far too much time and energy thinking about her mom and what she had and hadn't done and that small statement from a stranger struck a chord deep inside of her. The wall to her emotional dam cracked and split open, flooding her system with anger, regret and resentment. Tyce was right—Carol hadn't tried. She hadn't attempted to get better, hadn't tried to be a mom. While Lachlyn knew that depression was debilitating and soul-sucking, she also knew that Carol hadn't made any effort to feel better, to do better. The full bottles of antidepressant medication and empty boxes of sleeping tablets had told that story well. She'd wanted to stay sick and so she had.

Instead of fighting the negative emotions like she normally did, Lachlyn let them wash over her, knowing that they would pass. And when they did, a few minutes later, she felt cleaner for the dousing, able to see that understanding and relief were waiting to soothe her, a warm bath as opposed to a raging torrent.

Your mother should be very proud of you...

Had she lived, would her mom be proud of her? Lachlyn wasn't sure. She'd been so consumed by her illness, so wrapped up in being ill. She should have been there for her, she should have tried harder to get better, she shouldn't have let her down over and over again. But Lachlyn was still standing. *You have to let go of her*, Lachlyn told herself. *You have to, finally, say goodbye to her and your childhood.*

Ninety-nine out of a hundred women would've fought their illnesses to be there for their kids, and the same number would've stormed into their daughter's bedroom and kicked some young jerk's ass for laying a finger on her.

And while she was on the subject of parents, Connor might not have been able to restrict himself to one woman, but everyone she'd met had told her that he was an honest man who'd loved his life. He'd had an enormous capacity to love and he'd taught that to the children he'd raised as his own. He'd taught them to be kind, to be fair, to be committed, and that family was the rock you built your life upon. She wanted the Ballantynes to want to be her slab of rock.

So why was she being so damn stubborn about letting them in? Why had she avoided men and any type of relationship that smacked of emotional intimacy? Because she judged people based on the actions of a depressed, lonely, selfish woman, and that wasn't fair. To herself or to the family who wanted to claim her as their own. She was more like her mother than she wanted to admit. Instead of hiding behind her depression, she was hiding behind her independence, using her fear of leaning on others as a barricade against feeling anything.

*Enough. Enough now.*

Lachlyn, standing in that basement, a night cleaner dozing behind her, punched a mental fist through that thinking and decided that she wanted to live a full life. She wanted to be like her real dad who'd embraced life, who treated every day as a gift and an adventure. She wanted to love deeply and widely, to open herself up to the good and bad of life.

She needed to be honest about herself and what, and whom, she wanted in her life. Poor, rich or anything in between, she wanted the Ballantynes in her life. She couldn't wait to be able to walk into The Den and toss her coat onto the chaise longue next to the door, as was their habit, and count coats to see who was hanging out downstairs. She wanted to have more girly nights with Sage, Tate, Piper and Cady, to be hugged by her brawny brothers.

She wanted to watch Tyce's children grow up within a healthy environment, watch as they were taught to juggle their privileged life with service to others, and maybe teach her and Reame's…

Ah… Damn.

Lachlyn laced her hands behind her head. Reame was part of what she wanted, probably the biggest part of what she imagined her new life to look like.

He was already an integral part of the family, even
more than she was, and it felt right, so very right,
for the two of them, together, to be the last cogs in
the Ballantyne wheel.

Yes, she'd avoided men and relationships for fear
of being disappointed, but a sliver of her soul insisted
that she had been waiting for him, that her heart had
known what it was looking for and had decided to
be patient. Reame would never cheat on her or let
her down; once he made a commitment he stuck to it
like superglue. With her issues, she needed that dog-
gedness, his unfailing and deep-seated commitment
to what he believed in.

She needed him…

Lachlyn dropped the photograph and closed her
eyes, wrapping her arms around her waist. *Love* was
such a small word for what she felt for him. She
thought that when she finally fell in love, her world
would seem rosier, light-infused, celestial. It was
just… Lachlyn searched for the word…*real*. Loving Reame felt real. It didn't feel perfect or easy
or without its challenges. Her truth was that she'd
rather be beside Reame in a violent storm than safe
and warm by herself.

"Hey, I'm back."

Lachlyn jerked her head up to see her long-legged,
broad-shouldered man amble into the room. *Her*
Reame. His hair looked like he'd spent the evening
running his hand through it and his tie was pulled
away from his open collar. Golden stubble covered
his jaw and his eyes sliced through her like a hot

blade through butter. He slammed to a stop, his eyes narrowing and color leaching from his face.

Oh, God, he knew. Somehow, maybe because he was the other beat of her heart, he knew that she was in love with him, he knew what was in her soul.

And, judging by his tight mouth and tense jaw, he didn't welcome her silent declaration.

"You've made a decision about the family," Reame stated.

Lachlyn felt her knees soften and gripped the table, relief surging through her. He hadn't discerned her feelings of love, instead he assumed that the emotion in her eyes was a result of her deciding to be a part of the Ballantyne family.

Thank God. This way she could still be with him and pretend that they were friends who were having sex. She might even get to sleep with him again…

If she told him the truth, he'd run. They'd start avoiding each other and when they had to attend the same Ballantyne family functions, she'd be forced to endure stilted conversations with him across the dining table at The Den. Reame didn't want a relationship, he'd told her that often enough. Was it fair to burden him with her feelings, especially since the result of that conversation could affect the rest of the family?

She didn't think so.

"What's going on, Lachlyn?"

Reame's hard voice yanked her back and she quickly shook her head, then nodded toward the wingback chair. Greta looking wide-eyed and nervous, had yet to move from her seat. She looked even grayer than she did before. "Hold on, Ree."

Lachlyn walked over to her desk and, after scanning the list of extensions taped to the wall, picked up her desk phone and punched in a number. "Security? This is Lachlyn Latimore-Ballantyne. Can you contact the supervisor in charge of the cleaning staff and tell him that I have instructed Greta to go home, as she is ill? Also, I want you to call a cab to take Greta home."

Greta let out a low wail and Lachlyn disconnected the call. "Miss Lachlyn, I can't..."

Lachlyn went down on her haunches and rested a light hand on Greta's knee. "You have to go and get well, Greta."

"It's just me and my two girls. I have to work. I need the money. If I am away for too long, I might lose my job."

The hell she would. Lachlyn was not going to allow that to happen. "I will talk to my brothers and, between us, we will make sure that does not happen." Lachlyn looked at Reame, who was now looking bemused. "Reame, would you mind helping me with Miss Greta?"

Reame stepped forward and gently helped the older woman to her feet. He held her elbow as she started to shuffle to the door. He tossed a look over his shoulder and the corners of his mouth quirked upward. "You coming, Miss Latimore-*Ballantyne*?"

The man was as sharp as a spear, Lachlyn thought, picking up her bag. She was going to have to be very careful around him.

\* \* \*

Reame parked his SUV in his allocated space and looked at Lachlyn's exquisite profile in the low light of the car's interior. It was late and probably not the best time for this conversation—it had been a long and weird day—but he wasn't the type of guy who shoved his head in the sand.

He needed to know who, what and how and he needed to know now. And when it came to what was going on in Lachlyn's head, he needed to know *yesterday.*

Lachlyn started to open the door but he hit the lock button, effectively jailing her inside the car. She turned to look at him, resignation on her face.

"You're not going to give me any time to work this through, are you?" Lachlyn asked.

Reame shook his head. "Not when I suspect that whatever you have decided will have a big impact on my friends, personally and professionally."

"You're assuming that impact will be negative," Lachlyn said, sounding hurt.

*Dammit.* He half turned to face her and rested his hand on the knob of the gear shift, idly stroking the soft leather, wishing that he was stroking her skin instead. No, they needed to talk more than they needed sex. In fact, maybe they should hold off on having sex again anytime soon—the connection he'd felt earlier that evening terrified him. It was the first time he'd felt completely lost in a woman's touch. Lachlyn had swept him away. He needed to find some perspective and some distance and he couldn't do that if she slept in his bed, if she climbed beneath his skin.

God help him if she told him that she was falling for him. The quick, almost hopeful thought flittered through his brain and he quickly dismissed the notion, partly because the thought of Lachlyn loving him was fantastic and he shouldn't be feeling that way. As he'd watched his mom fall apart after a quarter century of loving the same man, he'd vowed that he would never put himself at the emotional mercy of another person's love.

His friends thought he was so damn brave for the work he did in the hot, war-ravaged regions of the world but Reame thought that, compared to love, war was easy. No, being brave was loving someone, forging a commitment, bearing the responsibility of making someone else happy. His dad had failed that acid test—he might, too. Yeah, sure, he was scared of being hurt like his mom had been, but what if he was just like his dad and couldn't be a good husband and father?

He refused to do that to Lachlyn…the only person who'd ever tempted him to think of what-ifs and maybes.

"Are we going to sit or are we going to talk?" Lachlyn demanded.

Right. Reame snapped out of his reverie and ran his hand over the back of his neck. "So, tell me what happened tonight."

Lachlyn drummed her fingers against her thigh.

"I think I am going to accept the Ballantynes' offer. I think I want to be part of their family."

Okay, that wasn't a huge surprise. The only one who hadn't been convinced that she'd find her way into the family was Lachlyn herself. "Want to tell me what prompted your decision?"

Reame wished that she would look at him. Her eyelashes were dark smudges against her cheeks, and she'd chewed off any remaining lip gloss hours ago. Emotionally exhausted, she looked more beautiful than he'd ever seen her. "I decided to let go of my past and my mother," Lachlyn said, her soft words dropping into the silence between them.

Reame waited a beat before covering her hand with his and interlocking their fingers. "I need more than that, Lach."

Lachlyn turned so that she was fully facing him, her thigh on the seat and her foot tucked under her opposite knee. She rested the back of her head on the window and pulled her bottom lip between her teeth. She looked both defiant and terrified, pissed off and…sad. Yeah, so sad.

"Our mom was hard work, Ree. She was chronically depressed but no matter how often she went to the hospital and the clinic, she never took her medication for longer than a month, maybe six weeks if we were really lucky. When I was young, she managed to work, just. By the time I hit my teens, she faded in on herself, doing the bare minimum to get through the day for the bare minimum wage. Her biggest ambition was to get home as soon as she could so she could pop a couple of sleeping pills and fall asleep as fast as possible."

His father had been a useless dad but he, at least, had been there. He'd interacted with his children.

"Tyce was amazing," Lachlyn continued. "He quickly realized that if he didn't do something, we'd either end up on the streets or in the system. He hustled for extra cash and, because he was always out beating the wolf away from the door, I was left alone. A lot." Lachlyn's eyes flashed and she held up her hand. "Don't pity me, I was fine. I spent a lot of time in libraries."

Reame just picked up her hand and rested his lips on her knuckles before placing it palm-down on his thigh, anchoring it, and her, with his much bigger hand.

"One day—it was around six in the evening and my mom had already gone to bed—I heard someone knocking on the door. It was a kid I knew from school."

Her voice had changed, Reame realized. It was now flatter and harder. "I had a bit of a crush on him so I let him in."

"How old were you?" Reame asked, hoping the sick feeling in his stomach wasn't warranted.

"Fourteen, nearly fifteen. He asked to see my room and as soon as he entered the room, he slammed the door shut and lunged for me."

Reame knew that he had to maintain control, that if she saw the rage on his face, she'd bolt. And he needed to know what happened, who the guy was, because that kid was now an adult and Reame would love to track him down.

"Did he rape you?" Reame asked bluntly, wincing at his own blade-sharp voice.

Lachlyn quickly shook her head and Reame felt a knot or two in his spine easing. "No, nothing like that. He kissed me and copped a few feels, and I was yelling like a banshee."

"Why didn't your mom—" Reame started to ask and his words drifted off. "She didn't hear you because she was asleep."

"The walls were paper-thin. You could hear a cricket sneeze," Lachlyn snapped. "No, she was either too medicated or she heard me and didn't give a damn. That night changed everything for me."

Of course it did. "Being sexually assaulted would."

"I told you, the boy didn't get that far. I'm not trying to excuse what he did but his actions didn't cause me to shut down. I don't want you to think that I avoided having sex because of him, either. I got plenty far with plenty of guys."

"Not what I wanted to know," Reame growled, the thought of another man's hand on her causing a fine red mist to appear behind his eyes. *This is not the time to feel jealous, moron.* "Did you at least report the assault?"

Lachlyn refused to look at him and Reame gripped her jaw and gently lifted her face. "Lach? Please tell me that you reported him?"

Lachlyn pursed her lips. "You're the first person I've told, ever."

*Crap.* Reame dropped his hand and felt like he'd been punched by an iron fist. *What. The. Hell?*

"Are you insane? That was attempted rape!" Reame roared.

"Calm down, Reame," Lachlyn said, clearly rattled. "It was an attempted something but I handled him, without my mom's help! And that's the point that I'm trying to get to!"

Reame reined in his temper, knowing that if he continued to imagine some little reject's sweaty hands on a young Lachlyn, he might put his fist through the windscreen which would a) hurt and b) cost a fortune. He took a couple of deep breaths and nodded for her to continue.

"Up until that night, I wanted a family, I desperately wanted a big, loud happy group of people who loved me and whom I loved. My mom's nonreaction to me being in danger, her lack of a response, hurt me so much that I decided, there and then, that a family couldn't be trusted to be there for me, that a family caused more hurt than anything else. I decided to go on my own, to isolate myself, to rely on myself and only myself. I refused to be a helpless little girl anymore."

Reame's heart wept for the young girl who'd lost all her dreams and her faith in humanity in one fell swoop.

Lachlyn took a deep breath and he saw the light of determination in her eyes, a strength of purpose that he hadn't seen before. Frankly, it turned him the hell on, which was totally inappropriate given the circumstances. "Tonight, I realized that I was done with giving my mom, and that night, so much power over my life. I wanted a family. I *still* want a family. I've been offered one, a spectacular one, and it's time I sank or swam. I've decided to swim, to become a Ballantyne. It feels right."

It was right. She had Connor's enormous capacity to love—she'd just buried it for a long time. When she forgot to be shy, to keep herself insulated, she was funny and outgoing and a little wacky, in the best way possible. She was just like her dad.

Lachlyn pulled in a deep breath and Reame saw her chest rise. He looked into her determined face, saw the resolution in her eyes and knew that she was about to drop another bomb in his lap. "Since I'm spilling my guts here, I might as well keep going."

Reame wanted to beg her not to. He didn't want to hear what she was about to say, because he instinctively knew that whatever it was would change something between them.

"As you know, I never had sex with anyone before you. Not because I was scared of sex or because I was a prude or because I wanted to save myself for marriage. None of the guys felt right and I didn't feel enough for them for the intimacy sex requires." Lachlyn sounded like she was carefully picking her words and each one dripped acid onto his soul. He didn't want to hear this. He didn't want to deal with whatever she was thinking, feeling.

"I knew, within hours of meeting you, that you were the one I wanted to make love to." Lachlyn tried to smile. "You're the only one I ever want to make love to…"

"Jesus, Lachlyn," Reame groaned. "Don't do this, please."

"Don't do what?" Lachlyn cocked her head. "Tell you that I think that you are incredible, that I think we could be good together? That I'd like to explore this to see where it goes?"

Reame felt a surge of anger. Why did women always do this? It didn't matter how clear you were, how simply you explained the situation, they always, always thought they could change your mind! He didn't want a relationship! Hadn't he told her that repeatedly?

How dare she spring this on him? How dare she try this female BS on him?

But underneath the anger, the fear, something hot and bright and exciting ran through him at the thought of them trying to create a family within the bigger family they were both such an intrinsic part of.

The delight and hope that thought raised made him scared, and when he felt fear, he always, always went on the attack.

Reame gripped the steering wheel, his knuckles white in the low light of the car. "Okay, let's go through this again," He said, keeping his voice bored, flat and sarcastic. "I told you that I couldn't sleep with you, that you were a job and nothing more. When we did sleep together, I told you that I wasn't interested in the responsibilities a relationship brings, in being at someone's beck and call. I told you, over and over, that I don't want a relationship!"

Lachlyn, instead of reacting to his anger, just looked at him, her amazing eyes steady on his face. She nodded. "Okay."

Okay? What did that mean? "That's all you're going to say?" Reame demanded.

Lachlyn's eyes cooled. "Did you think I was going to beg you to be with me? Did you think I was going to cry because you said no? Okay means that I get it, that I hear you, that I absolutely and unequivocally accept that you are uninterested in anything more than sex."

Reame felt like he was standing on quicksand and sinking fast. He'd totally lost control of this conversation. "Uh—"

Lachlyn tugged on the door handle. "Would you mind letting me out of the car now?"

Reame, not knowing what else to do or say, unlocked the car and watched as Lachlyn grabbed her bag and exited his vehicle. Following her to the elevator, he noticed the tension in her back, and when she turned, her normally vibrant face was blank and expressionless.

"I'll stay here tonight but I'd appreciate it if you could arrange for me to return to The Den. Linc and Tate are back and they have repeatedly said that they are happy to have me. If you still feel it's necessary for me to have a PPO, I'll take whoever you suggest." Lachlyn's hard eyes pinned him to the floor. "And I will pay for his or her services."

Over his dead body...

He couldn't leave it this way. He didn't want to lose her, dammit. He didn't want anything to change. He liked her, he loved the sex, enjoyed having her hang around his house. Days without her would be bleak but he couldn't give her what she was asking for. "Lachlyn, look...it's been an emotional couple of weeks. Maybe you're just a bit confused about what you feel...about me and about the Ballantynes."

Lachlyn whipped around and slapped her hand onto his chest. "Don't!"

Reame jerked back as her yell reverberated throughout the cube. It was the first time he'd ever heard her raise her voice and he took a precautionary step backward. Lachlyn closed her eyes for a brief moment and when she opened them again his knees nearly buckled at the emotion he saw bubbling in those dark blue depths.

"Just don't, Reame," Lachlyn said, her tone defeated. "For the first time in fifteen years I am seeing my life and myself clearly and if you keep talking, I might be tempted to start believing you. Because it's easier not to love. It's easier not to be involved. It's easier not to make an effort. I have been taking the easy route all this time and I'm done with it. So you don't love me, you will never love me, and you know what? It's okay, I can live with it. I learned a long time ago that you can't make someone love you— they either do or don't. I never begged my mother to love me and I certainly won't beg you."

The elevator doors opened and Lachlyn pushed

an agitated hand through her hair, tears in her eyes but refusing to let them fall. "Don't worry about me, Reame, I will be fine. I always am."

With those words whipping his soul, Lachlyn walked into his hallway and straight into the spare room, the sound of the lock engaging signifying that she was done talking.

Reame rested his open palm and then his forehead on the door, thinking that he'd maybe lost his only chance to be spectacularly happy.

# Twelve

Standing by the window of the formal reception room in The Den, Lachlyn used one finger to pull aside the sheer drape to check to see if there was a long-limbed, broad-shouldered blond man walking down the pavement toward the building. Nope. Still no Reame.

A day after leaving Reame's apartment, accompanied by a burly, noncommunicative PPO named Jack, she'd sent a message out on the family group chat, asking the Ballantyne family for a meeting, at a time convenient for them, to discuss her future. Reame was part of that group and while her head told her that he wouldn't intrude on a private family meeting, her heart wished he would.

She missed him terribly. They'd only been apart a few days but her heart was a ball of dough being pushed through a pasta machine. She wished that there was a way for them to be friends, to have some sort of platonic relationship and maybe, sometime in the future, they could. But not now, not when she wanted what her siblings had: love, affection and, judging by their heated looks, spectacular sex lives.

Reame hadn't lied to her, he hadn't led her on and she could blame nobody but herself for her state of misery. She shouldn't have slept with him, shouldn't have fallen in love with him. He was the one person she should've kept her emotional distance from. But then she would never have known him, heard his deep laugh, been able to look behind that superhero facade to the stressed-out man behind it, seen what an amazing friend he was.

Lachlyn straightened her shoulders. She missed him but she did not regret a minute she'd spent with him. He'd done so much for her. Aside from teaching her how amazing sex could be, he'd moved her into his apartment, helped her see herself and her past more clearly.

She'd love to have any kind of contact from him, but he'd have to make the first step. Hearing footsteps behind her Lachlyn allowed the drape to drop. Today would not be that day. Pity, she thought he might enjoy what she had to say. Lachlyn smiled at Linc entering the room. She accepted the kiss he dropped on her temple. "Are you sure you want to do this?"

Lachlyn nodded.

"Okay, then." Linc frowned and rubbed his thumb over the blue stripe under her right eye. "Still not sleeping, Lach?"

"Not really."

"Reame?"

Reame and Linc were childhood friends, best friends. She was not going to come between them so she'd never badmouth him. Not that she had anything bad to say about him. He didn't love her and wasn't interested in anything more than a hookup. That she wanted more was her problem, not his. "Nothing about this is his fault, Linc. In fact, I'm the one who's to blame."

Linc frowned. "I love Reame like a brother but I have never met anyone more stubborn, and that's saying something because I have Jaeger and Beck as brothers."

"Still, I don't want you blaming him for any of this," Lachlyn insisted. "And actually, I'd like you to do something for me, if you would."

Linc nodded so Lachlyn picked up her bag from the chair where she'd dumped it earlier and pulled a small box out of its depths. Nervous, she handed the box to Linc, who flipped open the lid. Lachlyn ran a finger over the unusual band—meteorite, amber and platinum—and remembered Reame's face as he'd examined the ring on his balcony just two weeks back. "I know you gave this to me and I don't want to sound ungrateful but Reame loves this ring. He loved your Dad—Connor—and I'll never wear it. But he might."

Linc didn't say anything so Lachlyn tried to tug the ring from his grasp. "Sorry, I've offended you. You gave me the ring and I should keep it. Just forget I said anything, okay?" she gabbled, her face flushing.

Linc snapped the lid closed before shoving the ring into the inside pocket of his jacket. He smiled at Lachlyn, wrapping a strong arm around her shoulder. "I love you because you are Connor's, Lach, but better than that, I like you. You are a rather amazing human being."

Lachlyn felt tears burning the back of her throat and she rested her head on her brother's shoulder, content to stand next to him and soak up his strength, because God knew, she would need it for the days and weeks ahead.

Despite recording the Ballantyne siblings' interview on the city's most watched morning chat show, Reame had no intention of watching it. He didn't need to know, as most of the city did, the intricacies of the financial settlement that the Ballantynes came to with their new sister.

He'd resisted temptation for two solid days before cursing himself to hell and back and pulling up the segment. He skipped through the footage until he saw Lachlyn and leaned forward in his chair, drinking her in. She wore a reddish-pink sheath that skimmed her tiny body and a matching shade of lipstick. The stylist had made her normally smooth hair look a little edgy and he liked it. Her eyes looked, as they always did, endlessly wide and deeply blue. Sage sat on one side of her and Linc on the other and, zooming in, he could see the fine tremble in her fingers.

She was terrified but hiding it well.

He should have been there, Reame realized, he should've been with her in the green room, rubbing her back, trying to distract her. He should have been standing off to the side, beyond the cameras, in her line of vision so that she could have an anchor, someone to talk to beside the pretentious interviewers and the cold cameras.

He hadn't been there because not only was he a scared wuss but a crappy friend. But being Lachlyn's friend was out of the question. He liked her, was possibly in love with her, but he didn't trust that what they had could last, that a relationship with her would stand the test of time. It was too big of a risk.

Being alone was, as she'd said, so much easier. Cowardly, but easier.

"So, tell me about the money."

Sage took Lachlyn's hand and squeezed it in encouragement and none of the Ballantynes leaned forward to answer the interviewer's forthright question. Lachlyn cleared her throat and Reame held his breath, feeling inordinately proud that she was stepping up and claiming her place as a Ballantyne.

"We're not prepared to go into details about personal family business, Lora, but my siblings and I have decided to start a foundation to support children from low-income families who live with parents suffering from depression. Apart from my work as the Ballantyne archivist and historian, I will be running the foundation, with the help and support of my siblings."

Reame swallowed the emotion in his throat. He could read between the lines: the money they'd offered her as part of Connor's estate would be channeled into the foundation. Linc would've only done that if Lachlyn accepted that she was part owner of the other Ballantyne assets. Linc would've also insisted that she take a cash settlement.

God, he was proud of her.

So proud that she could grasp love when it was offered to her, that she could look fear in the eye and kick its ass. He could keep his cool on the battlefield, fire and be fired upon, but he, despite his medals for bravery, didn't have a fraction of the courage his woman did.

Reame felt acid burn a hole through his stomach. Yeah, he loved her, he was pretty sure he did, but love wasn't enough.

He wanted a goddamn guarantee. He pointed the remote control at his TV and viciously jammed the button, replacing Lachlyn's exquisite face with a black screen. And if he couldn't get one of those then what was the point of sitting in his empty apartment feeling miserable? He might as well go out and try to find a distraction.

It wasn't going to work, he knew this, but he grabbed his coat and keys and headed out anyway.

Hours later, in a club called Burn, Reame took a tiny sip of the whiskey he'd been nursing for two hours and told himself to go home. He wasn't having any fun and the bartender kept sending him dirty looks for taking up a prime space on the corner of the bar. The strobe lights felt like they were slicing his brain.

He was tired, he was miserable but he didn't think he could go back to an empty apartment. He'd rather sit here and people watch and bat off occasional requests from women to buy him a drink or dance.

Reame felt movement at his elbow and the sweet scent of clean hair drifted over his shoulder. God, not another one. "Thanks but I'm not interested," he said, not bothering to look over. Eye contact always led to more conversation so he didn't bother.

He just wanted to sit here and get hammered. Unfortunately, getting hammered also required more than two drinks in two hours.

"Please, as if I would be interested in buying your sorry ass a drink."

Reame spun around on his chair to see Sage leaning against the bar, her Ballantyne eyes on his face and, worse, deeply unhappy with him. He looked around for Tyce, didn't see her tall, ripped husband, but did see the very pregnant Piper and the just-a-little-less pregnant Cady waddling toward him, causing the crowds to part. Tate followed in their wake.

Reame groaned. "What the hell are you doing here?" he demanded, after Sage ordered soft drinks and wine for Tate.

Sage cocked her head to the side and sent him a slow smile that shriveled his balls. "Well, we decided to come and help you with your quest to have wild sex with a wild woman."

Yeah, right. And he just saw a purple pig flying past. Man, his friends had very big mouths, Reame thought. And the only woman he wanted to make love with wasn't here.

The pregnant fairies reached and flanked him, dropping kisses on his cheek and staking their claim. Even if he did want to pick someone up, there was no way anyone would be brave enough to push their way through the barrier the four Ballantyne women had created around him. Good thing that sex with a stranger was the last thing on his mind.

Sage jammed her sharp elbow into his side. "There's a blonde eyeing you at ten o'clock."

Reame had noticed and dismissed her. "Why are you here?" he demanded, knocking back his drink and ordering another. "And how did you find me?"

"GPS locator on your phone. You know how Linc likes to know where all his chickens are," Sage replied.

"And we're here because our men think that they should stay out of your and Lachlyn's business," Tate added, frustration lacing her voice.

He agreed but he was smart enough not to say that aloud.

Sage poked her fingernail into his bicep. "They have all conveniently forgotten that they'd all needed help to get the fabulousness that you see before you."

Reame grinned. The Ballantyne women were pretty fabulous.

"Personally, I think that they are just a little scared of you and your Special Forces skills," Piper said, climbing up onto a bar stool and holding her enormous belly. Reame eyed it, worried.

"You're not about to go into labor are you?"

Piper looked at her expensive wristwatch. "In a few hours."

Reame felt the blood drain from his face. God, he was so dead. Jaeger was going to kill him. Then the four witches exploded into raucous laughter and he knew he'd been had. When they stopped cackling, Piper told him that he was safe, she still had six weeks to go.

"Twins. Bigger than normal," she explained between waves of laughter.

*Thank God.* "Not funny," he muttered.

"Oh, it so is," Sage replied. Then her face sobered and she walked to stand between his legs, holding his face in her hands. "You, however, are not. Why are you doing this to yourself? Why are you doing this to Lachlyn? Any fool can see that you are perfect for each other. Whenever you're together the air crackles. You love her, she loves you."

"I don't love her," Reame said, his heart cracking on that huge lie.

Sage dropped her hands and folded her arms, tapping her foot. It was a sign that she was getting mad and he tried to avoid Sage when her temper was up. "Fine. Then go and pick up that blonde and take her home for some wild sex."

Dammit. She had him there. "Don't want to do

that, either." Reame ran a hand through his hair and decided to be honest. "Look, I'm just scared that what I'm feeling now, what I could feel if I let myself, won't last. That one day I'll wake up and she won't be in love with me and I won't be in love with her and we won't feel what we are feeling now."

Four wise sets of eyes looked at him with complete compassion and heartfelt acceptance. Tate leaned forward and placed her cool hand on his arm. "Because of your folks?"

"Yeah," Reame said, his voice gruff. "My mom, she collapsed in on herself. I don't want that to happen to me or Lachlyn. She became a shadow of herself and I don't want that for us, either."

Sage wrinkled her nose. "I know your mom, Reame, and you know that I love her but, God bless her, she's not the strongest branch on the tree. Your dad took care of her, you take care of her, she's never had to make a decision in her life. Lachlyn is fully capable of looking after herself and if you did split up later she'd cope. It would suck but she'd be okay. You're the toughest guy I know, so you'd be fine, too. Using your mother as a yardstick is not a good idea, bud."

Reame was still trying to process her wise words, when Cady spoke for the first time. "Reame, you are also forgetting that love isn't just a feeling, it's a choice. When problems or tough times appear, the giddiness of love evaporates. You have to choose love. You have to choose to ride out a temporary lack of feelings, and believe that when the problem resolves itself—through honest communication and hard work—they will return."

That made sense, Reame thought, hope sliding into his soul. If he took their advice, he could almost, maybe, start thinking about approaching Lachlyn, about taking it slow, not looking too far into the future.

Tate opened her bag, shoved her hand inside and pulled out a small black box. She tossed it into the air and Reame snapped his fingers around the velvet square. "What's this?"

Tate shrugged. "No idea. Linc-the-wuss asked me to give this to you." The song changed, the volume increased and Tate's attractive face split into a wide smile. "Oh, I love this song. Who wants to dance?"

Cady and Piper both nodded enthusiastically and Reame sent them both an anxious look. "No labor-inducing moves, okay? Please? I'm on my knees begging here."

"No promises," Piper said as she walked—waddled—away.

Reame was considering yanking them from the dance floor—how, he wasn't sure—when Sage bumped her shoulder into his. "Open it, Ree."

Reame sent another look toward the dance floor, saw Piper and Cady swaying gently and Tate dancing like a mad woman, and then looked down at the box in his hand. He lifted the lid and saw Connor's ring, the one piece of jewelry he'd always loved. His heart tried to climb out through his ribs, and he fell utterly and completely in love.

"She loves you, Ree," Sage said softly.

"I know. I love her, too," Reame replied, taking the ring out and sliding it onto the ring finger of his right hand. It stuck at the knuckle so he tried the ring finger of his left hand. It was a perfect fit.

"Yeah, that works," Sage said, sliding her hand under his arm and linking her fingers with his. Sage sent him a sappy smile. "So what are you going to do about it?"

"Something. But not tonight." Reame sighed, knowing that he had to get his friends' women home safely before he could pursue his own.

Sage looked at the dance floor and then raised a cocky eyebrow in his direction. "You do know that they are going to be out there for hours, right? Or until Piper's water breaks," Sage said, amusement lacing her voice.

*Shoot me now.*

Sage tugged his hand. "Come on then, we might as well dance."

Reame slid the empty black box into his jacket pocket and sighed. Might as well, he thought.

"This building is a renovated prewar condominium. This particular apartment is sixteen hundred square feet and the ceilings are at ten feet. There are tilt-and-turn windows, oversize and facing north and east."

Lachlyn walked across the hardwood floors in the empty apartment to stand by one of those turn and tilt windows. Tuning out her Realtor, Marla's, voice, she started envisioning the space as an expansive lounge and dining room. Still, this condo building on the edge of Midtown wasn't where she wanted to be.

The Den wasn't ideal, either. She loved her new family but needed her space. She could go back to her apartment in Woodside but that wasn't practical. Her apartment was too accessible, she was still mad at Riccardo and she didn't want to go back to having a thirty-minute commute to work.

She needed, wanted, a place in Manhattan. When she'd agreed to officially become a Ballantyne, Linc had been surprisingly intractable about the financial aspects of their deal. Yes, he'd agree to a portion of the forty million being funneled into the Latimore-Ballantyne Foundation but she had to keep at least 50 percent for herself. She would also receive dividends from the company, director's fees and if they sold any assets, a fifth of the proceeds. Her bank account was ridiculously healthy and she could afford to buy a swish apartment anywhere in the city.

She'd looked at over twenty apartments and none of them had caught her fancy. Lachlyn knew that was only because they weren't on the top floor of the Jepsen & Associates building a dozen blocks from here.

"There's a sound system that runs through the house," Marla said, and Lachlyn tried to look like she cared. Judging by Marla's eye roll, she failed on that score and the real estate agent walked back into the hall.

Gripping the edge of the open windowsill, she closed her eyes and ordered herself to find her enthusiasm. Reame didn't want her with him, he didn't want anything from her—including her friendship— and the sooner she wrapped her head around that fact, the happier she would be. Well, she'd start the process to becoming happier...

This was a pretty apartment, Lachlyn thought, forcing herself to look around. Light, airy, new. It was probably the best she'd seen and she could come to like this place if she wasn't so hung up on that other place.

And that man.

"What do you think, Jack?" Lachlyn called out, knowing that Jack was standing in the hall guarding the door. She didn't expect a reply; in a week Jack had said less than ten words to her.

"I prefer mine."

*Reame.* Lachlyn's heart flew up her throat and a great shiver racked her body from tip to toe. Her instinct was to turn around and fly into his arms, but she kept her back to him, her eyes staring, unseeing, out the window.

"Yours isn't available to me," Lachlyn whispered, aching. "What are you doing here, Reame?"

Lachlyn heard his footsteps on the bare floor and then he was standing next to her, his back to the window, so close she could feel his heat. Lachlyn lifted her eyes to look into that face she loved so deeply and her eyes connected with his, but, as per usual, she was unable to read the emotion churning in all that green.

"Hi," Reame said softly, sitting down on the sill,

his hand gripping the edge, his pinkie finger intertwining with hers. Lachlyn felt sparks run up her arm and across her shoulder blades and it took all her willpower not to jerk away from him.

"Hi."

"As for what I'm doing here," Reame said, his voice low, "I have a few things to say to you."

He probably did, but nothing she really, really wanted to hear. "Okay."

"Firstly, congratulations on establishing the foundation and on doing that TV interview. That couldn't have been easy and I'm proud of you."

Lachlyn nodded. Yep, that she'd expected. Now he would say thank you for the ring and he'd wander out of her life again. Could she stand it? Did she have a choice?

Reame didn't speak for a long time and Lachlyn was tempted to fill the awkwardness with inane chatter. She held back and eventually Reame pushed his hand through his hair before rubbing his chin. "You are so much braver than I am, Lach. I am in awe of you."

Lachlyn frowned at him, utterly surprised. "But you're the soldier. You got the medals and everything."

"I have no problem risking my body, but my heart? Not so much. Until you, it was easy to dismiss love, to say that I didn't want it, that it wasn't worth the risk." Reame's finger tightened around hers. "But it's so worth the risk, Lach. You are worth the risk."

She was terrified to trust what she thought he

was suggesting. Lachlyn searched his face for an answer and saw his love for her in his eyes. "I love you, Lachlyn, whether you are a Latimore or a Ballantyne. Whoever you are is the person I want to be with, wherever you are is where I want to be. Is there any chance of you forgiving me for being a moron and giving me a second chance to see where this goes? Your pace, your choice."

Lachlyn rested her forehead on the ball of his shoulder, completely overwhelmed. Words of love bubbled in her throat but burst as soon as they hit her tongue.

It took her a while to string some words together. "About this apartment."

Lachlyn felt tension run through Reame's body and his shoulder slumped beneath her forehead, as if he were disappointed. Lifting her head, she kissed the side of his jaw. She couldn't wait another moment to embrace their happy…

"I hate this apartment and every other one I've looked at because it doesn't have you in it. I want to fall asleep in your arms, wake up to your smile. I want you to be my best friend, my lover, my emergency contact number."

Reame wound his arms around her waist, pulling her between his legs and tucking her into his chest. "Your husband? Any chance of that happening? I already have the ring."

Reame lifted his left hand and she saw Connor's ring on his wedding finger. She did a small, excited dance. "You're wearing the ring."

Reame smiled and Lachlyn's heart rolled over. "It's the only finger it fits. I thought about taking it off but since my heart will only ever belong to you, what's the point?"

Lachlyn felt her eyes prickle and burn. "Will you take it off for our wedding day when we say our vows?"

Reame held her face in his big hands, looking younger and softer and happier than she'd ever seen him. "Yeah, I can do that." His thumb caressed her bottom lip. "I suppose you'd like a ring, too?" he teased.

Lachlyn smiled. She pretended to think. "Man, I wish we had a gemstone hunter and a jewelry designer in the family."

Reame laughed. "It would help if we knew of anyone who owned a jewelry store or two."

Reame's mouth curved against hers and his kiss was full of promise, a taste of the future. Emotion whirled and swirled and Lachlyn felt an irrational burst of fear, thinking that if she didn't step back now, she never would. Old habits, she thought, pushing the fear away. *You're not going to spoil this moment.*

But she still felt the need to pull away from Reame, to look him in the eye. "It's not going to be easy, Reame. We're not easy people."

Reame nodded. "I know that but I don't want easy, Lach, and neither do you. I promise to fight for us, to surf every wave big enough to drown us. I need you to do the same. I don't want easy. I've had easy.

I want multidimensional, I want real, I want every layer and level of you."

*Oh, God.* Words to buckle her knees, to melt her heart. Lachlyn curled her arms around his neck and stood on her tiptoes to push her nose into the side of his throat, to inhale him, wishing she could step inside him. Her words, by contrast, were small and succinct. "I love you, Rec. So much. Always."

Reame stroked her back. "So, does that mean that you're not buying this apartment?"

Lachlyn stepped back, her eyes welling with happy tears. "I still need a place to stay."

"Funny, I know a place…"

Lachlyn smiled. "Does it have room for a body-guard?"

"Sweetheart, trust me, I intend to guard, and worship, your body for the rest of my life."

# Epilogue

**W**alking down the stairs to The Den, Lachlyn lifted the material of her chiffon dress—as close to the shade of Reame's eyes as she could find—so that the hem didn't drag on the floor. She peeked over the bannister to see the entire Ballantyne clan, formally dressed, filling the ridiculously big hall.

Outside, four limousines were waiting to transport the family to the Forrester Hotel where they, as a family, were hosting a spring ball to raise funds for the Latimore-Ballantyne Foundation. It was also her and Reame's informal engagement party and, unlike that ball she'd attended three months ago as a newbie Ballantyne, she didn't feel like she was walking up to the executioner's chopping block.

Before walking down the next flight of stairs, she took a moment to look at her family. Apart from the next generation of Ballantynes, everyone important to her stood in the hallway of The Den. Tyce and

Sage, her baby bump looking like a bowling ball under her designer gown. Her Ballantyne brothers, hot and urbane as they traded insults in a way that was all affection and pure habit. Tate, effortlessly beautiful. The new mothers, Cady and Piper, neither one looking like they'd recently given birth, Piper to twin boys and Cady to a red-haired little girl.

Her eyes danced over her family, love and affection filling her up and making her feel a little sappy and a lot grateful. She almost didn't want to look at Reame, because if she did emotion would get the better of her. Happy tears would slide down her face and she'd ruin the makeup she'd spent far too much time applying. But she couldn't *not* look at him. He was the beat of her heart, the pull of the moon, the bedrock of her life. Reame stood at the bottom of the stairs, looking ludicrously hot in a plain tuxedo and black tie. Reame's eyes darkened and she knew what he was thinking because, well, she was thinking it too.

*Let's blow this off and go back to bed.*

Lachlyn grinned and rolled her eyes—silently praying they never lost the passion between them—and Reame smiled, warming her from the inside out. Resuming her descent down the stairs, she held his eyes, so happy to be walking to him, into his arms, so grateful to be loved by such a spectacular man. Pulling her eyes from Reame, she flicked a glance at Connor's portrait and blew him a mental kiss.

*Thanks, Dad. I wish I knew you.*

Connor's voice, low and amused, drifted through

her head. *You do know me, Lach. I'm Linc's capability, Jaeger's adventurous spirit and Beck's big brain. I'm Sage's creativity and I'm your bravery.*

Before she could process his words, Lachlyn felt the air move next to her, saw the streak of pajamas passing her at full tilt. Shaw released a banshee yell as he flung himself off the stairs into fresh air. Again.

Reame stepped up, snatched Shaw out of the air and tossed his godson over h is shoulder. Lachlyn rolled her eyes but, as per usual, none of the Ballantynes batted so much as an eyelash.

As she tucked herself inside Reame's side, Lachlyn felt compelled to look at her dad's portrait again. She felt Reame kiss her hair, her temple. "All gorgeous, always mine," he said softly.

Connor would approve, Lachlyn thought. He'd loved Reame so much. She looked at his painted face again—the masculine version of hers—and furiously blinked away her happy tears. Then Connor's deep voice drifted through Lachlyn's mind again.

*Think of me as the Ballantyne guardian angel. I'm in you, with you, around you, always protecting you.* Then she heard her father's long-suffering sigh. *That being said, it pains me to admit that I might not be able to keep up with Shaw. That kid runs faster than I can fly.*

\* \* \* \* \*

# COMING NEXT MONTH FROM

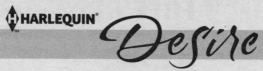
## HARLEQUIN Desire

### Available June 5, 2018

## #2593 BILLIONAIRE'S BARGAIN
*Billionaires and Babies* • by Maureen Child
When billionaire Adam Quinn becomes a baby's guardian overnight, he needs help. And his former sister-in-law is the perfect woman to provide it. She's kind, loving and she knows kids. The only complication is the intense attraction he's always tried to deny...

## #2594 THE NANNY PROPOSAL
*Texas Cattleman's Club: The Impostor* • by Joss Wood
Kasey has been Aaron's virtual assistant for eight months—all business and none of the pleasure they once shared. But the salary he offers her to move in and play temporary nanny to his niece is too good to pass up—as long as she can resist temptation....

## #2595 HIS HEIR, HER SECRET
*Highland Heroes* • by Janice Maynard
When a fling with sexy Scotsman Brody Stewart leaves Cate Everett pregnant, he's willing to marry her...*only* for the baby's sake. No messy emotional ties required. But when Cate makes it clear she wants his heart or nothing, this CEO better be prepared to risk it all...

## 2596 ONE UNFORGETTABLE WEEKEND
*Millionaires of Manhattan* • by Andrea Laurence
When an accident renders heiress Violet an amnesiac, she forgets about her hookup with Aidan...and almost marries the wrong man! But when the bar owner unexpectedly walks back into her life, she remembers everything—including that he's the father of her child!

## #2597 REUNION WITH BENEFITS
*The Jameson Heirs* • by HelenKay Dimon
A year ago, lies and secrets separated tycoon Spence Jameson from analyst Abby Rowe. Now, thrown together again at work, they can barely keep it civil. Until one night at a party leaves her pregnant and forces Spence to uncover the truths they've both been hiding...

## #2598 TANGLED VOWS
*Marriage at First Sight* • by Yvonne Lindsay
To save her company, Yasmin Carter agrees to an arranged marriage to an unseen groom. The last things she expects is to find her business rival at the altar! But when they discover their personal lives were intertwined long before this, will their unconventional marriage survive?

---

**YOU CAN FIND MORE INFORMATION ON UPCOMING HARLEQUIN® TITLES, FREE EXCERPTS AND MORE AT WWW.HARLEQUIN.COM.**

HDCNM0518

# Get 4 FREE REWARDS!

## We'll send you 2 FREE Books plus 2 FREE Mystery Gifts.

**Harlequin® Desire** books feature heroes who have it all: wealth, status, incredible good looks... everything but the right woman.

FREE Value Over $20

---

*A year ago, lies and secrets separated tycoon
Spence Jameson from analyst Abby Rowe. Now, thrown
together again at work, they can barely keep it civil. Until
one night at a party leaves her pregnant and forces Spence
to uncover the truths they've both been hiding...*

*Read on for a sneak peek at*
*REUNION WITH BENEFITS by HelenKay Dimon,*
*part of her JAMESON HEIRS series!*

Spencer Jameson wasn't accustomed to being ignored.

He'd been back in Washington, DC, for three weeks. The plan
was to buzz into town for just enough time to help out his oldest
brother, Derrick, and then leave again.

That was what Spence did. He moved on. Too many days
back in the office meant he might run into his father. But dear
old Dad was not the problem this trip. No, Spence had a different
target in mind today.

Abigail Rowe, the woman currently pretending he didn't
exist.

He followed the sound of voices, careful not to give away his
presence.

A woman stood there—*the* woman. She wore a sleek navy
suit with a skirt that stopped just above the knee. She embodied
the perfect mix of professionalism and sexiness. The flash of bare
long legs brought back memories. He could see her only from
behind right now but that angle looked really good to him.

Just as he remembered.

Her brown hair reached past her shoulders and ended in a
gentle curl. Where it used to be darker, it now had light brown

highlights. Strands shifted over her shoulder as she bent down to show the man standing next to her—almost on top of her—something in a file.

Not that the other man was paying attention to whatever she said. His gaze traveled over her. Spence couldn't exactly blame him, but nothing about that look was professional or appropriate. The lack of respect was not okay. As far as Spence was concerned, the other man was begging for a punch in the face.

As if he sensed his behavior was under a microscope, the man glanced up and turned. His eyebrows rose and he hesitated for a second before hitting Spence with a big flashy smile. "Good afternoon."

At the intrusion, Abby spun around. Her expression switched from surprised to flat-mouthed anger in the span of two seconds. "Spencer."

It was not exactly a loving welcome, but for a second he couldn't breathe. The air stammered in his lungs. Seeing her now hit him like a body blow. He had to fight off the urge to rub a hand over his stomach. Now, months later, the attraction still lingered…which ticked him off.

Her ultimate betrayal hadn't killed his interest in her, no matter how much he wanted it to.

If she was happy to see him, she sure hid it well. Frustration pounded off her and filled the room. She clearly wanted to be in control of the conversation and them seeing each other again. Unfortunately for her, so did he. And that started now.

*Don't miss*
*REUNION WITH BENEFITS by HelenKay Dimon,*
*part of her JAMESON HEIRS series!*

*Available June 2018 wherever*
*Harlequin® Desire books and ebooks are sold.*

www.Harlequin.com

HDEXP0518

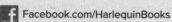